MW00463688

THE SWALLOW MURDERS

THE SWALLOW MURDERS

•

E. L. Larkin

AVALON BOOKS
NEW YORK

PRINTED IN THE UNITED STATES OF AMERICA
ON ACID-FREE PAPER
BY HADDON CRAFTSMEN, BLOOMSBURG, PENNSYLVANIA

This one is for my two girls, my most faithful readers.

Chapter One

My first thought as I turned into the long curving drive was that I had no idea Birdie's family was so well off. Anyone who could keep up a place like this had to have money, a lot of it. The glimpses of the front lawn I caught through the rhododendrons looked more like a well-tended golf course than a private residence.

What the—I'm going to hit her! was my next thought as I rounded a curve and slammed on my brakes.

A child dressed in tennis shorts and a tank top was lying in the middle of the drive, her out-flung arms and legs giving her the appearance of a discarded doll.

Twisting the wheel frantically, I crashed into the bushes, skidding to a stop inches from the child's feet. The adrenaline rush made my heart slam against my ribs and for a moment I thought I was going to be sick all over my new Dockers.

As soon as my knees would hold me, I stumbled out of the car and had just taken a step toward the child when a woman strolled out onto the drive from a path between the trees.

1

She stopped, blinked, and started screaming.

At the same time a young boy came racing out from behind a huge forsythia bush, howling with laughter. He was followed by still another woman who came around the curve of the drive, took one look at the situation, and gave the boy a wallop on his behind that almost knocked him off his feet. She then proceeded to give the body a kick in the ribs, sending it sailing across the drive where it impaled itself on a low-hanging branch.

I sagged onto a fender and gaped at her.

"For heaven's sake, Allie, shut up," the kicking woman shouted at the other, still-shrieking woman. "It's only that stupid blow-up doll Junior gave him."

She aimed another wallop at the boy's fanny. She had him pinioned by one arm, but he managed to twist away from her and raced up the drive, still laughing like a hyena. Allie, who had quit screaming, followed him.

The body gradually deflated into a limp plastic nothing. After looking at it for a long minute I said, very loudly and clearly, "That kid needs to be taught a lesson, and if I ever get my hands on him I'll sure as heck do it."

"I hope not," the woman said. "His father is a lawyer and the boy is his pride and joy."

"I don't give a flip if his dad is a Supreme Court justice," I snapped. "He nearly gave me a heart attack. To say nothing of my car."

"I can't say as I'd blame you but I'd advise against it," the woman said in a neutral tone. "You must be Birdie's friend Demary Jones. She told us about you at breakfast. Which is what gave Buddy the idea, of course. Do you think you have any real damage?" She motioned at the Toyota.

I turned to scowl at it. The adrenaline in my system

was gradually subsiding but my insides were still churn-
ing and I was getting madder by the minute. I have a
short fuse to start with and I not only had the stuffing
scared out of me, but this woman's casual acceptance of
the boy's hoax really ticked me off. I hadn't been going
over five miles an hour and had hit mostly low-growing
shrubs so the Toyota probably hadn't sustained anything
more than a few scratches, but I very easily might have
plowed into one of the larger trees and been seriously
injured.

"I am sorry," the woman said, reading my mind. "You
could have been hurt. And I will see that Buddy learns
the error of his ways. My name is Ruth, by the way. I'm
one of Birdie's aunts."

I didn't answer. I couldn't trust myself to be civil.

"Why don't you leave it there," she said, motioning
at the car again. "Come up to the house with me. The
walk will do you good and I'll send someone down to
check on the damage."

There wasn't much else I could do so I started up the
road beside her, deciding as I did that I didn't like her.
I never do like people who tell me what's good for me.

As it happened, however, she was right. By the time
we reached the front of the house I had calmed down
and realized that while Buddy needed a severe talking-
to he didn't need to be strung up by his thumbs. I opened
my mouth to say so but before the words were out I
suddenly remembered why I was there.

I was supposedly delivering a package. A present my
old school friend, Birdie, actually Barbara Swallow, had
asked me to drop off on my way to Bellingham where I
was taking the Alaska ferry the next morning.

"It's a special gift," she had told me. "It has to be
there tomorrow, but her address is so out of the way even

FedEx won't guarantee delivery by tomorrow morning. And I can't go myself until the weekend."

That was three o'clock yesterday afternoon, Wednesday. How could Birdie have told them all about me at breakfast? What was going on here? Why hadn't she brought the present herself? The house wasn't even a half hour from the Wallingford district of Seattle where we both lived. And what had she said about me to inspire Buddy's trick?

My thinking had gotten that far when Birdie came flying down the front steps and threw her arms around me. "Demary, are you all right?" she cried. "Allie just told me what that beastly kid did."

"I'm fine." I returned her hug without enthusiasm, still wondering what she'd told her family. Birdie can get some wild ideas in that curly-haired head of hers.

"Honestly, that boy of yours is terrible," she said, glaring at Ruth.

Ruth said something I didn't catch and went on into the house.

"Buddy is her child?" I demanded, starting to get mad all over again.

"Yes, but he really isn't her fault. I mean, the way he behaves. His dad has custody. She got little Ellen and he got Buddy."

It took me a moment to sort that out. Birdie's mind works faster than her mouth—or vice versa—and it frequently takes a quantum leap to catch her meaning. How she manages to hold down her highly complex job as a cost accountant is beyond me.

"Come on in now and meet Gran and—"

I pulled my arm out of her grasp. "No, I'm not going to come on in. Not until you tell me what I'm doing here. Obviously you didn't need a package delivered. What's in it, anyway? Crumpled-up newspapers?"

"I wouldn't do that," Birdie said, sounding hurt. "Gran's birthday present is in it."

"So?"

Birdie avoided my eyes, staring at her shoes, her fingernails, down the drive. "Oh, all right," she said finally. "I did fib because I wanted you to meet Gran." She looked at me eagerly. "Demary, when you talk to her you'll see what a doll she is. You won't believe what those silly psychiatrists say. I know you claim you aren't a PI but you do have a private investigator's license and—"

I stopped her in mid-flow. This was sounding worse by the minute, a typical Birdie mishmash. I do own and operate C.R.I., Confidential Research and Inquiry, which at one time was a private detective agency. It isn't now. "Barbara Swallow, I am not a PI and you know it," I said sharply. "I'm a researcher and a genealogist. Now what did you tell your family? And why do you want me to talk to your grandmother?"

"Oh, Demary," she wailed. "You just have to help me. Everybody in the family says Gran killed Grandpa and his girlfriend but I know she didn't. I just know it!"

"How old is your grandmother?" I asked. Not the most pertinent question but it was the first thing that popped into my mind. I had a mental vision of a trio of geriatrics trying to shove one another down a flight of stairs.

"Gran's seventy-six but Grandpa was fifty-five when . . . What difference does it make how old she is?"

"None. I don't really care and I don't even want to see her, but out of sheer curiosity I would like to know this—if your Gran is seventy-six and your grandfather was fifty-five, how old was the other woman?"

"I don't know. Thirty maybe? She was a circus performer."

"I see. It must be in the genes. Birdie, I'm leaving—now!" I started back down the drive. Despite considering Birdie certifiably loony, I was very fond of her. But I wasn't about to take on her entire family of aptly named birdbrains.

Chapter Two

I marched off toward my car—trailed by a determined Birdie—saying I would not listen to her, and anyway, what in the world did she expect me to do? Birdie is gentle and unassuming but when she has her mind set on something she has all the flexibility of a brick wall.

"If you'll just listen I'll tell you," she wailed.

"Birdie, you listen to me," I said firmly, coming to a stop and turning around to face her. "I am not a detective. Just because I've had some accidental luck figuring out a couple of cases for friends doesn't mean I—"

"Aren't I a friend?" she interrupted. Tears began to trickle down her cheeks.

"Of course you are," I said, feeling mean. "But Birdie, I can't get involved in a murder case out here. I'm not a detective and I'm not a psychiatrist. This is Snohomish County jurisdiction and whoever is in charge of the case, doctor or police, would be furious if I stuck my nose—"

"Oh, no," she interrupted again. "Nobody will care. It was all settled twenty-two years ago."

"What was settled twenty-two years ago?" I asked, confused.

"The murder, Grandpa's murder. And Dian's too, of course, although the coroner said it wasn't at the same time."

I gaped at her. "Your grandfather was murdered twenty-two years ago and they are just now arresting your grandmother?"

"And Dian too, don't forget."

I shook my head in a vain attempt to clear it. "Never mind Dian. Let's just stick with Grandpa. Why now, after all this time, are they arresting your grandmother? Have they found new evidence?"

"Oh, no. They never did have any evidence, they just arrested her because she acted so crazy. But she isn't— wasn't—it was just shock. They were going to put her in Steilacoom—you know, the state nuthouse—but Junior persuaded them to let him keep her in Windsor House. It's a private place. That's how come she's come home now. Junior got Windsor to let her out in his custody because of the diary."

There was a concrete bench a couple of feet away under a big magnolia tree. I backed up and sat down. "Birdie, come sit down beside me and answer my questions. Just my questions, understand? Don't start off on any explanation of your own. Okay?"

"All right." She followed me docilely. We sat facing each other.

"Now, first, your grandpa was killed twenty-two years ago. Right?"

"Yes, but so—"

"Just my questions, remember? So, when did they arrest your grandma?"

"I'm not sure but I think it was about three weeks after they found him. Grandpa, I mean."

"Three weeks after . . . You mean they arrested her twenty-two years ago?"

"Yes, but—"

I held up my hand, stopping her. I thought maybe I had it straight. "The investigation pointed to your grandmother but instead of a trial she was committed to an institution. Right?"

"Yes."

"Okay. Now who is Junior?"

"He's my uncle. Mom's brother. Mom's the oldest, but Junior is a lawyer, so—"

I shook my finger at her. "Wait, we'll get to that. So Junior has recently uncovered some evidence that points to her innocence and has persuaded the authorities to let her out in his custody to—"

"Oh, no. He just talked Windsor into letting her out for a little while."

"Little while? Did he go get her this morning? Does she have to be back this afternoon?"

"I don't think so," she said vaguely. "She's been home for more than a week now."

I sighed, wondering if the whole family was demented. "All right. So Junior got her out and she's home for a *while*. Why? Her birthday?"

"No, because of the diary Alison found in the desk she wanted."

"Diary? Whose diary? And where did she find it?"

"Gran's diary, and I just said where. It was in a desk she wanted."

I decided this wasn't going to get me anywhere except more confused. I obviously wasn't asking the right questions.

Birdie waited, gazing at me hopefully.

"Okay, let's try another way," I said. "You just start with Grandpa's murder and I'll ask the questions as we go along."

"Yes, yes, that's best," Birdie said eagerly. "Twenty-two years ago, right at this time of year, June, one of the neighbors, Mr. Johnson, asked if he could use the big chest freezer Gran kept in the shed. She said yes and when he went to open it up he found Grandpa and Dian in it."

"I presume dead?" I said sourly.

"Of course," Birdie said seriously. "Anyway, the police came and pretty soon they decided Gran did it on account of Dian having an affair with Grandpa. Gran said she didn't do any such thing and Dian wasn't his girlfriend either. But then in a couple of days she started acting so weird they decided there was no use in having a trial, and they were going to put her in Steilacoom."

"And then your uncle persuaded the authorities to put her in Windsor House instead. Right?"

"Yes, and she's been there ever since until a couple of weeks ago after Alison found the diary. That's when—"

"Hang on a minute," I interrupted. "Who did you hear all this from, Birdie? Twenty-two years ago you were just a kid. Ten, twelve years old."

"Mom told me some of it. And we've always gone to visit Gran at least once a month. Mom doesn't think she killed anybody, either. She doesn't even like talking about the murders but everyone does anyway. Not when she's around, though." Birdie stopped and thought a moment. "She gets really mad when anyone starts wondering, out loud, how Gran did it."

"Yes, that's an interesting question," I interrupted again. "How did she kill them?"

"That's just it, she didn't. How could she? They were both bludgeoned to death with a piece of pipe. It was in the freezer with them. She couldn't do that. She couldn't have gotten them into the freezer, either. She only weighs about ninety pounds and Grandpa was a great big guy. Dian was no lightweight either."

That sounded more logical than most of Birdie's statements. "Okay, let's jump now to this diary that Alison found in a desk. Where was the desk? And who is Alison?

"Mom's sister. Gran had three children. Mom, Junior, and Aunt Alison. Aunt Alison was the one doing the screaming when Buddy pulled that stupid trick with the doll. She thought it was Ellen. He put Ellen's clothes on it." She stopped to make sure I understood and at my nod went on. "The desk was in the attic. It was all dirty and cobwebby but Aunt Alison liked the shape of it. She didn't know it was Gran's then but when Junior brought it downstairs for her to clean she had him turn it upside down to look for spiders and she found the diary in a secret little drawer at the back underneath the other drawer, and. . . ."

Birdie rambled on for several minutes, with me trying to sort it out. I asked more questions as she went along, again sorting mentally as she spoke, and finally I thought I had the picture fairly clear. Maybe.

Twenty-two years ago Birdie's grandfather, Howard Martindale Swallow III, aged fifty-five, had been found in a big chest freezer alongside his supposed mistress, Dian Clark, a circus performer. The subsequent investigation pointed to his Rosellen as the guilty party but by the time the authorities reached that conclusion Rosellen was obviously unable to stand trial and she was installed in Windsor House.

Rosellen's son, Howard Martindale Swallow IV, known as Junior, was appointed trustee of the estate. This spring he had informed the rest of the family that they would have to sell the house because taxes, upkeep, and the cost of keeping Rosellen in Windsor House were exceeding the estate's income—income that came from one small, middle-class hotel in Everett and three commercial rentals in Seattle. Three weeks ago the family met at the house to pick out any furniture or bric-a-brac they wanted to keep for themselves. Alison decided she wanted the desk and found Rosellen's diary. Rosellen wrote in a kind of code of her own so most of the diary was indecipherable, but the last several pages, undated but presumably written just before she was taken to Windsor House, contained lines of figures. These figures corresponded, loosely, to sums of money that were withdrawn from her and Howard's joint bank account in the days between Howard's leaving the house—supposedly on a trip to San Francisco—and his body being found two weeks later in the freezer. The money, fairly large sums, had never been found.

What Birdie wanted was for me to prove her "Gran" innocent—she didn't seem to be particularly interested in finding the real killer—and to decipher the diary, as it was sure to hold all kinds of clues. Or so she assured me.

"Birdie, what you need is a cryptanalyst, not a genealogist. I can't even decipher a crossword puzzle," I protested.

"You do solve puzzles all the time with your research. Maybe not exactly like this, but still . . . And anyway, it's not the money I care about, I don't care if anyone ever figures out what happened to it. It's Gran I care about. She didn't kill anyone, I know it. Please help me. Please, please, please."

I took a deep breath, ready to tell her I couldn't begin to figure out a twenty-two-year-old murder, when a picture memory flipped into my mind's eye. I saw Birdie, who wasn't the ditzy blond she appeared, holding my hand, crying with me, the day my friend and employer, George Crane, was killed in a drive-by shooting. No big thing, maybe, but Birdie cared. The least I could do was spend a couple of hours meeting her Gran and taking a look at the diary.

Chapter Three

I naturally thought the meeting with Rosellen would take place immediately and I'd be on my way again within a couple of hours. It didn't work out that way. Rosellen had already eaten and had gone to her room to take a nap, so the meeting had to be postponed until later.

Lunch turned out to be serve yourself. Birdie took me into a huge kitchen where a sideboard was loaded with a selection of cold meats and cheeses, a tub of Kentucky Fried Chicken, three baskets of breads and rolls, and a big bowl of bananas, apples, peaches, and early pears. There were stacks of paper plates and a box of plastic eating utensils on each end of the counter.

"There are a couple of salads in the fridge and some cold drinks," Birdie said, handing me a plate. "There's something hot in the warning oven, too—lasagna, I think."

It was a perfectly wonderful kitchen in spite of the antique appliances and well-worn, yellow-painted cupboards. Sun poured in through the windows on two sides of the room. They were curtained in flowered polished cotton that matched the cupboards and the pale green tile countertops, the kind of place that practically called out for a woman in a ruffled apron. There was no sign of anyone actually using the kitchen, though. No pots of geraniums on the windowsill, no notes stuck on the refrigerator, and no small appliances such as a toaster or blender.

Birdie must have read my mind because she went on, "No one actually lives here anymore," she said. "But everyone in the family does use it for a vacation place sometimes. There used to be a housekeeper who came in but Junior let her go a long time ago. Once in a while Mom and Chuck and I come for weekends; the beach is just down there through the trees." She waved toward a line of trees and shrubs at the far side of the lawn that was visible through the big window at the west end of the room. "And no one wants to cook for this mob anyway, so Junior has a catering outfit bring all this in. They brought cereal and bagels and stuff for breakfast, too, but everyone has to fend for themselves."

"Works for me," I said, building a sandwich on a seven-grain roll. I wanted to get lunch over with, meet Rosellen, and get on my way. Besides taking the Alaska ferry up the Inland Passage the next morning, I also had some research I wanted to do in Bellingham before I left.

No matter what Birdie thought, solving a twenty-two-year-old murder that had already been investigated by the police was an exercise in futility. Most murders are at least well on their way to being solved within the first week. If you don't have a some idea of who and why by that time, the chances are you never will.

Out of friendship I'd give the diary a try. She might have written something vital in the way of tracing the money that had disappeared, but beyond that I had zero chance of solving anything.

I didn't say any of this to Birdie as we took our plates through to the dining room and sat down at a round oak table. Trying to change Birdie's mind about anything is a real exercise in futility.

The sun on the leaded glass doors of a big old china cabinet at the side of the room was sending shafts of glittering light around the room. It and a sideboard under the window were beautiful pieces of craftsmanship, with carved insets of grapevines and leaves on the corners and across the tops of the drawers. Too large and too heavy for most homes nowadays, the furniture fit this room as if it had been specially made for it.

We had almost finished our lunch when a big man came in from the hall. He wasn't fat, nor particularly tall, just big, and good looking without being actually handsome. He had bright blue eyes and a wide mouth.

"You must be Birdie's friend, Demary Jones," he said, smiling. "I see she has persuaded you to stay."

"Was there ever any doubt?" I asked. I meant the remark as a mild joke but the annoyed expression that washed across his face told me he didn't take it as such. I thought of apologizing but changed my mind. I didn't have anything to apologize for. Being here wasn't my idea.

"Demary, this is my Uncle Howard. Most everybody calls him Junior," Birdie said, speaking so faoost she almost stuttered. I wondered why he made her so nervous. He didn't appear threatening in any way.

Junior nodded pleasantly and went on toward the kitchen. At the doorway he turned and came back to stop beside the table again. "Miss Jones, I don't know what kind of story Birdie has been telling you, but there really isn't any case here for you to, ah, solve. The police made an exhaustive inquiry at the time and were satisfied that Mother committed the crime while of unsound mind. She is only home now, temporarily, because I was able to convince the people at Windsor House that I would keep a close eye on her. The lady with her"—he turned to Birdie—"is not a friend keeping her company. She's a psychiatric nurse."

"I knew that," Birdie murmured, her eyes on her plate.

"Hard as it was to accept, we all had to admit the police did a thorough job. Mother was guilty. And to speak frankly, we would rather not go through it all over again. Mother is calm now but if you stir everything up there is no way to predict what might happen. She could turn violent and this time I might not be able to keep her out of Steilacoom."

"I hardly think that looking at her diary will disturb her," I said blandly. "Birdie tells me she doesn't even recognize it as being hers." Despite his pleasant good looks and prosaic attitude he struck me as a man who could be a bully, and I wasn't about to betray Birdie to him.

He hesitated, looking taken aback. Birdie had told me he practiced corporate law and seldom, if ever, went to court, but his obvious annoyance made me wonder how successful he was. Most lawyers, or at least the only ones I knew, seemed to think maintaining an inscrutable expression was the prime requisite for success when it came to their profession.

"I do intend to meet her, though," I went on. "Only courteous, wouldn't you say? This is her house, isn't it?"

He stared at me silently for a good fifteen seconds before agreeing. Then, nodding politely, he left without saying anything more.

Birdie drew in a slow breath. "Don't say anything," she whispered.

In a moment the back door opened and closed. Birdie waited another moment and then got up to look out the window. "He's going over to Jordan's," she said, letting her breath out in a whoosh of relief.

"Why are you scared of him?" I asked.

"I'm not scared of him, it's just that he'll call Mom and yell at her if I do something he doesn't like."

"Call her? She hasn't joined the gathering of the clan?" I knew Birdie's mother, who was totally unlike her daughter, and I wouldn't have thought she would take being yelled at.

"She and Chuck are in Portland seeing Grandma Swallow. She's been sick. I saw her last weekend. You knew my dad was a third cousin with the same name, didn't you?"

I nodded. Birdie's father had been killed in Vietnam. Chuck was her brother, and I recalled now that Birdie had once told me that her mother had very little to do with her own side of their family.

"They are both flying back tomorrow evening and will be here Saturday morning for Gran's birthday party. It doesn't bother Mom when Junior yells at her, though; she just hangs up, or walks away, but it bothers me," Birdie went on. "He's mostly nice but I don't like him yelling at her."

I grinned to myself. Birdie didn't like yelling, period. She seemed to shrivel up when anyone raised their voice. I've always been a bit surprised that she and I have remained such good friends. I yell a lot.

M'Who's Jordan?" I asked. "Is he a relative, too?"

"Kinda. A distant one. His mother was Gran's second cousin. I think. He's a Wyndlow. Jordan Wyndlow. Gran was a Wyndlow. He does live here. Not in the house, in a little cottage place on the south side of the property. It faces on another street.

"Chuck and I were afraid of him when we were little but I think that's because he's a writer."

I blinked. "You were afraid of him because he's a writer?"

She giggled. "Don't be silly. Of course not. Anyway, I guess he should be called a poet, not a writer. Although he must have to write it down, doesn't he? Otherwise how would anyone know."

I decided I didn't want to untangle that. Instead I asked, "If he was here when you were a kid he must have been living here when your grandfather was killed. Yes?"

"Oh, yes, but he didn't know anything about it. Mom says he came here when she was in college. Gran told him he could stay in the cottage because he was writing an epic poem and needed a quiet place to work. He doesn't pay rent but he keeps the lawn mowed."

"Did he publish the poem?"

"I don't think so. I don't think he ever published any- thing." She paused, looking thoughtful. "Maybe that's why mumbles to himself all the time."

I decided to give it one more try. "Is that why you were afraid of him? Because he mumbles to himself?"

"No-o, not entirely anyway," she said, frowning. [11"He's so big, though, and he's got a loud, gruff voice that always sounds cross. And he has this funny beard that looks like the mice have been at it. Looking up at him when we were little was just scary."

That sounded like Birdie—she must have been born timid. "You said he was here when your grandfather was

killed but that he didn't know anything about it. Why do
you say that?"

"Well, he, ah . . ." She looked down, brushed some
crumbs off the table into her hand, and deposited them
neatly on her plate. "He, ah . . . well, he drinks."

I grinned. "That's too bad, but it isn't a crime. C'mon,
Birdie. What did he do?"

She sighed. "He was drunk and the police picked him
up and he was in jail and the woman, too, and he was
with her for a whole week. A whole week. And even if
they didn't know when Grandpa . . . when it happened,
they were pretty sure it was sometime that week."

"The woman was in the drunk tank with him for a
week?" That was impossible. Even back then they didn't
put men and women in the same cell.

"Oh, no. Not in the cell. And he was only in jail overnight. He was at her house for a week and the neighbors
complained because they were making so much noise.
They had a big party."

"For a week? That must have been some party. But at
least it gave him a good alibi. How about the rest of the
family? How many of them were around? And how were
their alibis?"

"Almost all of the family was here at one time or
another. Mom was and so was I. No one had a real alibi
except Jordan, because the coroner never could decide
exactly when they were killed."

Chapter Four

I frowned at her. "Why not? Why couldn't he tell when they were killed?"

"I don't know. Maybe because the neighbor, Mr. Johnson, left the freezer lid up and pulled the plug."

"Good grief! Why? He should have known better than to do that."

"Well, yes. He did. He said he was sorry but he was just so . . . so flabbergasted he didn't think. In fact, he said he meant to take them clear out but he couldn't, they were stuck in there, so he went home to call the sheriff."

"Well, they couldn't have thawed much in a half hour or so."

"No, of course not, but the coroner still couldn't tell definitely. He decided on a time and said it was within a week of the first of the month, either way."

My head was beginning to ache. Birdie frequently had that effect on me. Twenty-two years ago forensic science wasn't what it was now so, under the circumstances, they could have had a difficult time pinpointing the precise time of death. But that long a span?

"It has to be after he said because Grandpa was home on the fifteenth; his banker talked to him." She paused, then went on. "And I think the coroner said they weren't killed at the same time, either."

I ran my fingers through my hair, undoubtedly ruining the three-minute style I had created that morning. Not killed at the same time? She must be mistaken. It didn't make sense.

"What did your grandma say about all this?"

"She said Grandpa was in San Francisco on a buying trip. Grandpa had just bought the hotel and he was going to remodel it. But of course he wasn't. She was confused."

"M-m-m, yes. I'd say she was." And from the sound of things so was everyone else. *I* certainly was.

Rosellen came downstairs shortly after one o'clock. She was a perfectly darling little woman with a slender figure and an air of not quite being in the room. She had soft, fluffy white hair done in a messy chignon, sapphire-blue eyes, and the creamy complexion a twenty-year-old would have envied.

She was dressed in a type of shirtwaist dress that had been popular in the sixties, with a snug waist, flared skirt, and buttoned-down collar. Birdie told me later it was one of many dresses that had been left hanging in her closet when she was taken to Windsor House. It was made of a silky blue material that matched her eyes and swirled around her still very good-looking knees. She wore it with a certain panache that struck me as being at odds with her vague attitude.

Rosellen introduced the woman who came with her

into the big sitting room simply as Shirley, with no pretense of her being a friend, or anything else.

We three, Rosellen, Birdie, and myself—Shirley never said a word in my hearing—had carried on a light conversation about the weather for approximately two minutes when Junior came in. He was followed a minute or so later by Alison, to whom I was duly introduced. The weather discussion continued for another minute or so; we switched to children, proceeded to another apology regarding Buddy's trick in the drive, and were starting on family connections when it dawned on me that my mildly sarcastic comment to Junior in the dining room regarding meeting Rosellen was what was meant to be. I was to meet Rosellen, not talk to her. Or at least that was what Junior, and probably Alison, intended.

I didn't see any reason to frustrate them. I doubted if talking to Rosellen at this point would be productive anyway. From the very shrewd look I caught in her eyes a couple of times I didn't think she was any crazier than I was, or at least not at the present time. What she might have been twenty-two years ago, or even yesterday, was anybody's guess. But if she had not told Birdie anything about the events surrounding the murders, she wasn't going to tell me. Birdie was very obviously her favorite person.

The diary was something else and after Rosellen and her minder wandered off I asked to see it.

"Of course," Junior said with a polite, if somewhat strained, smile. It didn't take a high-octane brain to see he wished Birdie had never talked to me. However, he motioned to me to follow him, led me into a small, rather dimly lit room at the end of the hall that contained racks of bookshelves, mostly empty, and a large rolltop desk. The diary was in the top right-hand drawer of the desk, which he unlocked with a simple two-flange key. He removed and handed me the small book without comment.

It was a flat, cardboard-covered notebook, five-by-eight size rather than a regular diary, and appeared to have been hard used. The corners were blunted, several pages were crumpled, and the covers were stained and grubby.

After a minute I asked, "Do you mind if I take it into the other room? The ink has faded and it's not very light in here."

He hesitated, then said, "No, go ahead." He escorted me back to the sitting room. "Take all the time you like with it. I have some things I need to do in town. I'll be back in an hour or so."

Birdie, who was looking out the window, turned and stared after him as he crossed the hall to the dining room and turned into the kitchen. I tucked my arm through hers and started for the front door.

"Let's take a stroll around the grounds, I'd like to see the yard and I can see this better in the sunlight, too," I said, giving her arm a sharp tug. Alison had left and the sitting room was empty except for us but it had four doors, none of them quite shut, plus the archway to the hall, so there was no telling who might be listening. And I'd just as soon no one else heard me.

"What makes everyone think Rosellen wrote this?" I asked when we were out of earshot of the house.

"Her name is written on the first page," Birdie said, frowning. "Why are you asking that?"

"Did anyone ask her?"

"Junior did right away. She said she'd never seen it before but of course no one believed her. Even I didn't," she said, tears close to the surface.

"Don't go all weepy on me, Birdie. Get a grip."

She gulped. "All right. But why don't you think it's hers?"

"I didn't say I didn't believe it was hers, but it certainly isn't in character. She seems to me the type to be using a Morocco leather-bound volume with gold lettering, not this thirty-nine-cent job."

"They didn't have the kind of money for leather-bound things. Grandpa had mortgaged everything to the hilt to get the money to buy the hotel. Junior—"

"Oh, come on, Birdie. This place is worth a mint," I said, waving at the house and grounds.

She nodded. "That's why Junior wants to sell. But it wasn't when Grandpa was alive. In fact, I can remember when most of the grounds were nothing but weeds and some old fruit trees. Jordan is responsible for making it look so nice. He likes gardening and I think he likes riding the big mower around. But the rest of the place is falling apart." She turned and gazed back at the house. "Just look at it, Demary. The roof leaks, the chimney in the front room is leaning sideways, Junior says we can't have a fire in that fireplace until it's fixed, and nothing has been painted in years. The only central heat is an old coal furnace that doesn't even work anymore so it's impossible to heat the place in the winter, and it will cost mxore than a mint to have it replaced."

When I took a good look I saw that she was right. At first glance the house appeared to be a mansion but if you really looked you saw it was the grounds that painted the picture, not the house. And furthermore the house wasn't even all of a piece. What appeared to be the central part had been added on to several times and none of the additions had been well thought out. They didn't match the original structure.

Thinking back I realized that even the sitting room we had just left, a beautifully proportioned room with a gorgeous old Persian rug, was badly in need of refurbishing. Several off-color squares and oblongs on the walls showed where pictures had been removed. The rug, too, was shabby and threadbare in places, as were the drapes and upholstered chairs.

"Grandpa inherited the house from his grandpa in 1950. He, my great-great-grandpa, or whatever he was, bought the place sometime in the twenties. It was a farm then and wasn't worth much because it was too far from Seattle, or Everett, to live in if you were a working man, and what few roads there were out this way were dirt. I don't think waterfront property meant much then and it wasn't worth much as a farm either because it was too run-down."

"Why did he buy it, then?"

"He was a bootlegger. He ran booze from Canada by boat and landed it down there on the beach."

Chapter Five

Birdie pointed toward the line of shrubs beyond the back lawn. "I told you. The property goes clear to the Sound. The path is through those trees. It was just a sandy little cove then; the Amtrak right-of-way wasn't there."

I stared at her in disbelief. Birdie was positively the most conservative, straight-arrow, nonliberal person I've ever known. I would have thought admitting one of her grandparents was a bootlegger, and without even a quiver of apology, would be beyond her.

"Don't look at me like that," she said defensively. "I didn't have anything to do with it, and besides that everybody drank bootleg liquor in those days."

I burst out laughing. "Birdie, you are something else," I said, giving her a hug. "They did indeed and they probably considered your great-great a benefactor of humanity rather than any kind of lawbreaker."

Right then I decided the case I was working on would have to wait. I was going to figure out the diary and prove Birdie's Gran had nothing to do with any murder.

How I was going to do it was something I'd worry about later. First, I'd have to wrangle a weekend invitation out of Junior and that might not be easy. I had a feeling he wasn't too keen on my services. I wasn't sure why but I suspected that it was because if anyone deciphered the diary dollar signs he wanted to be the first to know, something he couldn't trust me on.

As it turned out I didn't have to depend on working my way into his good graces. When we went back inside Ruth, Junior's ex-wife, Buddy's mother, was in the hallway with a tray of glasses and a pitcher of lemonade. She offered us a glass and asked if I had made any headway on the diary. When I said I hadn't really had a chance to look at it she invited me to stay for a few days.

"At least until Sunday. We'll probably all be leaving then. Junior will be taking Rosellen back then, too. There is plenty of room here and it will give you a chance to really study the thing," she said pleasantly. "When you look you will see that parts of the writing have faded, or are covered with a musty kind of mold, but most of it is clear enough to make out the letters, if not the sense."

I accepted with alacrity and no one objected when I brought in my bag and Birdie installed me in the bedroom she was using where there were twin beds. Not even Junior, who saw us in the upstairs hall and asked what was going on. He didn't look happy but didn't argue about it, either. I learned later that Junior never ever disagreed with anything Ruth said or did.

"Why not?" I asked Birdie when she mentioned it as I was unpacking the few things I'd brought in.

She shrugged. "I don't know. He just doesn't. No one knows why she divorced him, either. But actually he doesn't argue much with anyone, 'cept Mom, and she says that's been going on since they were teenagers. She thinks it's because she's older than him and bossed him around a lot when they were little." She chuckled suddenly. "She left him in a packing case once."

"She what?"

"She was supposed to be watching him. He was about five at the time. She and a friend were playing cops and robbers and he was supposed to be the robber. The packing case was the jail. They ran off chasing more robbers, I guess, and forgot about him. When Mom went home without him Rosellen threw a tizzy but they found him safe and sound in his jail. He says he doesn't remember but I bet he does and that's why he yells at her every chance he gets."

I grinned. "Well, I have the same trouble with my brother, and I never left him in a packing case. And come to think of it, I have problems with Cissy, his wife, too. She tries to boss me around. It sounds as if Junior's divorce was friendly, at least. No trauma for the two children."

"I guess." She thought a minute. "It was funny, though. Not funny ha-ha, funny strange. They weren't having any trouble, nothing that anyone ever heard about, anyway. He just went home from work one day and she was gone, with both kids. Or so he said. He said she never even left a note but I think that's a lie; she wouldn't do that. No one in the family heard from her, though, until she filed for the divorce."

"Did another man, or woman, enter the picture?"

"No, nothing like that. I think he's seeing someone now but she isn't."

"What does she think about the murder?"

"She's never said. She didn't know Junior then or at least not very well but she must have seen him sometimes because she lived just down the beach from here.

Her dad was a caretaker at a condo place and Junior had a girlfriend there so he went swimming in their pool all the time. 'Course, Ruth was only eighteen then."

That took me a second to sort. "She seems to have stayed on good terms with the family, even Junior."

Birdie nodded. "Yes, mostly anyway. She's a nice person. I see her around quite a lot. She lives in our neighborhood, you know. She doesn't visit Rosellen but then she never knew her, and she doesn't like the kids to see her, either. But I can understand that. They're too young to understand why she's in Windsor House."

"Well, right now I've got to call Martha and have her do something about my ferry reservation tomorrow. May I use the phone? Is it hooked up?" Martha is my office manager, my secretary, my friend, and anything else she feels like being. Black and beautiful, she is an even six feet tall with a figure like a board, Grecian features, close-cropped black hair, and an astringent personality. Surprisingly, considering how timid Birdie is, the two get along great.

"Sure, the phone is downstairs in the library. Where Junior had the diary. But even Martha won't be able to do anything about getting you a reservation for next Friday. The Alaska ferry is always booked full months in advance."

"Well, maybe someone else will cancel like I'm doing."

Birdie looked unhappy. "I'm sorry, Demary. I never thought about you being on a job."

"Don't worry about it. It isn't that pressing and I can always fly." I had some people to see in Ketchikan and should have flown anyway. Much faster. Taking the Alaska ferry had been an indulgence. I'd always wanted to go up the Inland Passage and I wasn't on any kind of time schedule.

I'd been hired by a strange old tugboat man, Captain Sven Nordan, to do some research on the motor vehicle ferry, the *Kalakala*. He intended to write a private history about the beautiful art-deco ship that had plied the waters of Puget Sound from 1935 to 1967. Retired from state ferry service and purchased by American Freezerships in 1969, the ship spent the next twenty-five years grounded in Gibson Cove in Kodiak, Alaska, as a seafood processing plant. In November of 1998 the shining silver *Kalakala* had been raised from the mud and gravel of its stationary bed and towed back to its home port, Seattle. It was now in the process of being turned into a convention center and tourist attraction.

Martha didn't scold as much as I expected. Plus, she said she'd get busy seeing what she could dig up on the murder, which, knowing Martha, would probably be a lot. She can not only make a computer do all kinds of tricks, she is a perfect genius at persuading file clerks and the like to dig out information and fax it to her.

We talked for ten minutes or so but I didn't realize anyone else was on the line, listening, until I started to hang up. I'd said good-bye, thought of something else, told Martha to hang on a second, and heard the soft click of a third person replacing the receiver.

Martha heard it also. "Well, well," she said softly. "What cheek, that." Born in Barbados but raised in Liverpool, England, Martha came to the United States via Canada in the eighties but she still has a buttery English accent and uses English colloquialisms.

"I wonder who is so interested," she added. "Maybe you had better watch your back, Demary. The murder may be long gone in the past but that doesn't mean the villain is."

Chapter Six

I meant to start on the diary right away but it was such a beautiful day I decided to first take another look outside. We spent the next half hour strolling around the grounds while Birdie told me what she knew about the two murders. All of it hearsay.

The cottage where the murders allegedly took place was a converted motor-court unit that Grandpa Howard had purchased several years before his death and moved onto the property to use as an office. It was at the end of the path that led from the back porch around the corner of the shed where the big freezer had been kept and down toward the water. It was surrounded by overgrown shrubs and was almost invisible from twenty feet away. It was also in a state of complete ruin and was, in fact, boarded up.

"Junior had it boarded up as soon as the police finished with it," Birdie said. "He wanted to burn it but he couldn't get a permit right then because the weather was too dry and then I guess he just left it."

I poked around the outside of the little building trying

to look in the windows but between the boards criss-crossing them and years of grime nothing much could be seen. There were apparently two rooms with a small bathroom between. I could make out the remnants of a couple of chairs but nothing else.

"How did the police decide this was where they were killed?" I asked.

"The back room had a bed then. It didn't have sheets or blankets but Gran had put an old chenille spread on the mattress and they found it buried in the sand down on the beach. It had a lot of blood on it, plus they found blood on the mattress and spots on the floor, too."

"Blood from both of them?"

Birdie frowned. "I don't know. I think they both had the same blood type but I don't think they did any DNA tests or anything. Maybe they didn't have DNA testing then. Or if they did they didn't think they needed to do it."

That sounded pretty sloppy to me.

"So what made the police so sure Rosellen killed them?"

"Her fingerprints on the pipe."

I stopped trying to pull some branches away from the bathroom window and stared at her. "No fooling. That might do it for sure. You didn't tell me about fingerprints."

"I haven't had a chance. And anyway, it doesn't matter because Grandpa used the pipe to prop the door open and Gran had handled it dozens of times, so of course her prints were on it."

"Were there other fingerprints?"

"I don't know."

"What else?"

"What else what?"

"Birdie! They must have had other evidence. They wouldn't have judged her guilty on just that alone. What else was there?"

"Nothing. Truly. Except the way she acted, of course," she said, picking at a button on her shirt.

This was like trying to extract one specific jelly bean from a full jar. "How did she act?"

"Well, for one thing Grandpa had been gone for several days and she didn't report him missing. She said it was because he had gone to San Francisco but no one else ever heard him say anything about making a trip down there. And then, of course, it was the way she acted when the police said Dian was his girlfriend." Birdie hesitated, looking at her shoes. I waited. "She hit the detective with her purse, and tried to bite the policeman who grabbed her."

"Sounds reasonable to me," I said, straight-faced.

Birdie gave a reluctant smile. "I guess it wasn't reasonable at all. I wasn't there but I heard about it from Mom. Both she and Junior were with her at the police station in Everett. Rosellen threw a regular hissy fit, carried on something fierce. Mom said she was crying and yelling and calling the detectives names all at the same time."

"That still doesn't sound . . . Did she have a lawyer present?"

"Of course. Junior."

"Was he her lawyer all along? I mean, was he her only lawyer? Did he represent her through everything?"

Birdie nodded.

"And did he represent her at her competency hearing?"

"Yes. He did all of it. And it was a good thing, because Rosellen could never have paid a lawyer as good as he was. And besides, there was hardly any money to pay a lawyer at all."

"I thought he did corporate law, not criminal."

"He does now, but when it happened it wasn't too long after he passed the bar and he was still working for the firm where he'd interned and they took nothing but criminal cases. In fact, that's what he intended to do, according to Mom. He planned on going to work in the district attorney's office."

"I wonder why he changed his mind?"

She shrugged. "Whatever, it was a good thing he was still there. They helped him with a lot of the stuff he had to do. Pro bono. And of course the money was another thing the police had against Rosellen, and that's why all the fuss about the diary, too. The money that disappeared out of their joint bank account between the last time anyone saw Grandpa and when they found the bodies."

"How did it disappear? Drawn out in cash at the bank, checks, or what?"

"Telephone transfer and checks that had Rosellen's signature, but she said she'd never written them."

"How much?"

"Not a lot by today's standards but it was a lot then. Somewhere around twenty-five thousand dollars. I don't know the exact amount."

"Did a handwriting expert look at the checks?"

"Ye-es. I guess so. The man at the bank."

I nodded and started back toward the house. From the sound of things, neither the firm he worked for nor Junior had done too good a job for Rosellen. But, of course, that was just Birdie's version of what she had heard over twenty years ago. She could have it all wrong. I'd get a better idea of what went on from the official records, if I could lay my hands on them. Or rather, if Martha could, and I had every faith that she'd have them in hand Monday morning.

For now I was going to take a good look at the diary. I still had it in my jacket pocket.

I was no expert at decoding anything, including my own notes at times, and after studying the diary for less than fifteen minutes I knew I wasn't going to have any luck with it. For one thing, much of the writing was blurred. I could make out most of the letters but others were so scrawled or so dim they were simply guesses. And if you guessed wrong you would, of course, change the meaning. And on top of those difficulties it wasn't written in normal sentence structure. Some lines simply had eight or nine letters, there were no capitals and no punctuation. For instance, one line read, "s4cs cno lt 3oc" or it might have been "84cs ono ll 3oo" To the writer, presumably Rosellen, it would no doubt have some meaning but to me it looked more like reminders on a grocery list than anything else.

"Has Junior had any kind of a specialist look at this?" I asked. We were sitting at the little table in the corner of the kitchen. The sun, pouring in the window behind her, made a fluffy halo of Birdie's blond curls. Birdie looks the quintessential blond bimbo with her huge blue eyes, high color, and cupid's-bow mouth. You have to know her a while to know there's a brain behind the facade.

"I don't think so. Alison only found it a week ago. He did say something about getting it copied and—" She stopped with a little gasp. "Demary, nobody is around right now. Let's take it over to one of the strip malls on Highway 99 and find a copy place. Then you'll have plenty of time to figure it out. We can be back here before Junior knows we've gone. He probably wouldn't care, but still . . ."

That was an excellent idea. Not only would I be able to study it, I had a friend I'd gone to school with who more or less made a living doing this kind of thing. He lived in Denver but I could fax it to him. And not only that, I knew he frequently was consulted by the CIA, so he might have connections there who were good at deciphering stuff also.

We grinned at each other like a couple of idiot conspirators and twenty minutes later were in a copy shop having the entire diary photocopied. Twice.

With the murder twenty-two years in the past, it never occurred to me that we were being anything other than silly.

Chapter Seven

The family gathered in the big sitting room for pre-dinner drinks at six that evening. Dinner was the same as lunch—serve yourself—but someone had covered the dining room table with an embroidered cloth and set regular plates, napkins, and eating utensils on the sideboard in that room instead of in the kitchen.

The drinks were nonalcoholic except for two bottles of red wine. I settled for a bottle of designer water with a slice of lemon.

Alison's husband, George Davis, had joined the group as had Jordan Wyndlow, the caretaker. I was introduced to both and was amused to see that Jordan's beard did indeed look as if the mice had been at it. He was big, too, at least six foot four, with a harsh voice. He was perfectly courteous when introduced, but I could see why he had intimidated Birdie as a child.

"I checked your car over," he told me. "It seems to be in perfect condition." He raised his eyebrows slightly. "In fact in far better condition than a car that old normally is. The only damage I could see was a small scratch on the left-hand fender. We are all very sorry it happened, though."

I nodded. "No real harm done."

George, who attached himself to us as we were speaking, made me think of a mushroom, about the same shape and kind of spongy looking. He was seriously overweight with heavy shoulders and overhanging belly that narrowed down to bony hips and thin, almost spindly legs and small feet. He was wearing khaki shorts and a bright orange golf shirt that did nothing good for his appearance.

"Birdie tells us you're a private detective," he said, by way of opening a conversation. "What kind of detective work do you do?"

I wanted to say I snooped in political bedrooms—which would certainly be a lively topic—but decided not. "I think she meant I have a PI license," I said instead. "I don't actually do much of that kind of work. My degree is in research, and I do a lot of genealogy work."

"Research? That sounds intriguing," Alison said, joining us where we were standing by the window. "What are you researching at the moment? If it's not something you don't want to talk about." Her deliberate tone made research sound faintly unclean, as if I really did snoop in people's bedrooms, uncovering things that should be left well hidden.

"Oh, no, I love to talk about what I'm doing," I assured her, deciding to make what was really a fascinating story sound as dull as possible. "In fact I have a very interesting job I'm working on right now. A history of the *Kalakala*. I'm trying to document firsthand reports of some of the more exciting incidents in its history, such as the time in 1936 when it accidentally rammed the ferry *Chippewa*. The *Chippewa* had a forty-foot hole torn in its hull but the *Kalakala* was only dented. I'll be going to Alaska next week to talk to the son of one of the hands who were aboard at the time. He has a letter from his father that was written the day after the accident."

Alison gave me a blank stare. She must have been expecting something very different. "Isn't that an old ferry? The *Kalakala*?" she asked, frowning.

"Yes. Actually one of the most famous ships ever built. In its heyday it was known nationwide. Postcards featuring the *Kalakala* were seen all over the world."

"How, uh, interesting," she said as she wandered away.

I grinned to myself. Alison was one person who wasn't going to be interested in anything I might be doing. She obviously thought I was a dimwit, which was all right with me.

I'm a scant five foot two, with curly auburn hair, green eyes, freckles, and a rosy complexion, all of which tends to make me look like an over-the-hill Little Orphan Annie. My looks make ferreting out information ridiculously easy sometimes. No one takes an investigator seriously when she reminds them of a comic strip character.

Ruth and Birdie, who had been getting themselves something to drink, came over to stand beside me. Ruth nodded out the window. "I very seldom come out here anymore but I shall miss seeing all this when Junior sells the place. It's particularly beautiful in the early spring when all the rhodies are in bloom. The blooms are mostly gone now."

She had changed her clothes since I'd seen her earlier and was now wearing a tailored pantsuit in a dull citron shade that went particularly well with her dark hair and brown eyes. She was an attractive woman. The outfit was a little formal, however, for a family gathering and I wondered if she planned on going out later.

"I told Ruth what you said about the diary," Birdie said in a low voice.

"What? What did I say? And why are you whispering?"

She looked around nervously. "Well, I thought maybe you didn't want anyone to know yet. But it's all right to tell Ruth. She's leaving and she won't tell anyone."

Ruth smiled. "I think what she means is that I don't have any interest in it, anyway. But I do agree with you. I've only seen the thing once, and didn't take much of a look at it then, but that was the first thing I thought of, too. A list, not a diary." She made an uncertain gesture. "I've never kept a diary, though, so I'm no expert."

"Birdie said you were leaving?"

She nodded. "I have a dental appointment early tomorrow so I'm going home after dinner but I'll be back Sunday morning to pick up Ellen and Buddy. Alison said she'd keep an eye on them."

I had forgotten about the two children. "Where are they?" I asked, looking around the room. Everyone else appeared to be there including Rosellen and her minder, Shirley.

"They're having hot dogs at a bonfire down on the beach with some neighborhood kids and their parents," Birdie answered. She put her soda can down. "Let's make a sandwich and go down there with them. It's really nice out."

"Do you think your grandmother would like to go?" I asked.

Ruth gave me an assessing look. "Yes, why don't you ask her, Birdie? Shirley can go too."

                        *   *   *

It was a little cooler on the beach but we had brought
heavy sweaters for everyone, and the neighbors, Mr. and
Mrs. Lathrop, had built a huge fire. There seemed to be
an awful lot of kids for one family but as I learned there
were actually three sets of children. Buddy and Ellen
were there, as were three of the Lathrop children and
three more from another family on up the beach. One of
the latter was a teenage girl who was supposedly keeping
an eye on her two small brothers.

Birdie made her grandmother comfortable in the lee
of a log with Shirley alongside of her and put our picnic
basket on a blanket in front of her.

Rosellen had been delighted to come to the beach. She
seemed to view the simple outing as a bit of an escapade,
and as Junior had been out of the room at the time we
went along with the idea. We bundled our meal into a
basket, grabbed sweaters and blankets, and took off.
Again, Shirley said nothing. She simply came along. As
everyone was doing a lot of milling around, going in and
out of the kitchen, dining room, and sitting room I don't
think anyone actually saw we were taking Rosellen with
us. And with any kind of luck no one would realize she
wasn't upstairs in her room until we went back. Very
possibly no one would care, either, but I had a feeling
none of them, with the exception of Ruth, wanted me to
talk to her alone. And, of course, that was exactly what
I was hoping to do.

"It's so beautiful," she said with a soft sigh as I sat
down beside her. "I haven't been down here, or for that
matter, even seen the Sound for twenty-two years. I forgot how wonderful it is in the summer." She motioned
at the sweep of water in front of us. It was dotted with
boats of all sizes and shapes. The Ballard Locks were

not far south of us, around the curve of Meadow Point. Many of the boats were heading that way, to tie up at the big Shilshole marina or to go on through the locks and into Union Bay or Lake Washington.

Directly in front of us two forty-foot sailboats with their spinnakers set were racing each other for position. Farther out a tug was towing an immense log raft north toward Everett and the mills there. It was a beautiful scene with the sun sparkling on the water, the snow-capped peaks of the Cascade mountains in the distance, and the multicolored boats skip-dancing their way along.

I was glad we'd brought her down to the beach; I thought it was too bad the family had not brought her before. I didn't think we had done anything wrong, and certainly nothing dangerous. She clearly wasn't dangerous. She couldn't have weighed more than ninety pounds, and Shirley was a good-sized woman.

Danger, however, has many faces.

Chapter Eight

I finally got an opportunity to speak to Rosellen out of Shirley's hearing when we decided to move farther away from the fire. Rearranging blankets and food and all the rest of our gear somehow—with a little help from me—put Birdie and Shirley on the far side of the blanket from Rosellen and myself.

I didn't try to rush her. I had already seen it was difficult to get her to talk at all. Sometimes she didn't seem to hear or she chatted amiably about a book, or movie, or something she had seen, without any connection to what anyone else was saying or asking. I started out talking about the beach, the children, innocuous current events, and the new TV shows. None of which got much response. Eventually I asked, "Does the house look the same as it did when you lived here with Howard?"

She smiled faintly, not looking at me, her eyes on Birdie. "She was such a pretty baby. I knew she'd be beautiful when she grew up."

I gave up. I knew she heard me but if she didn't want to answer, or couldn't, there was nothing I could do about it, and it wasn't fair to keep at her. Just the one mention of Howard had left her soft face looking distressed and anxious.

"I don't really know any more," she said suddenly, several minutes later. "I remember my own room, but the kitchen is strange. And some of the furniture. I never saw that desk before." She turned her head and looked directly at me. "Sometimes I can't remember Howard, but I didn't kill him."

Her gaze slid off toward Birdie. "Can we have something to eat now?" she asked, her voice as sweet, and vacant, as her face.

The sun was just sliding behind the saw-toothed line of the Olympic Mountains across the Sound when we finished eating. Birdie was starting to gather up our debris, ready to stuff it back into the basket, when Rosellen got to her feet.

"I think I'll go wading," she said, starting to trot in the direction of the water's edge.

Shirley didn't call out, and she didn't seem to hurry at all, but she had a hold of Rosellen's arm before she was six feet away. She swung the smaller woman around gently and started back up the path to the house.

Rosellen said something to her but went along docilely. A moment later they were out of sight among the shrubbery.

The entire incident didn't take more than a half minute, but it left me shaken.

"Why can't she go wading if she wants to?" Birdie said, looking after them with a scowl.

"In her shoes and stockings?" I asked, very quietly. No one else seemed to have noticed the small scene and it was better that no one did, particularly the children.

"She would have taken them off," Birdie said in what for her was a sharp voice. "What did that woman think she was going to do? Run away?"

I didn't answer.

"What did Gran say to her? I couldn't hear."

"She said, 'Life is hard. It's easy to die.' "

"Wha-a-at?" Birdie gasped. "You think she was going to try to drown herself? Commit suicide?"

"I think it's an old Russian proverb," I said evenly. Which didn't mean suicide wasn't what she had in mind, but I didn't say so. I felt desperately sorry for her, and for Birdie. I could see why Birdie was so anxious for me to prove her innocent somehow; she was a sweetheart. And so helpless.

That night, on my way back to the bedroom after brushing my teeth, I heard Junior and Ruth talking in the bedroom next door to Rosellen's room. Actually, they were arguing but were keeping their voices down. I didn't really stop and listen but I did slow down to where an arthritic snail wouldn't have had any trouble passing me. I heard Junior's voice first.

"I won't do it, Ruth," he said. "I can't, she's my mother."

"What's important is you would probably lose your license," Ruth snapped.

"That's hardly likely at this point."

"Don't kid yourself, Howard. It's just as possible now as it ever was. She doesn't belong in Windsor House and we all know it."

Low as it was her voice held a kind of hostility that startled me. She didn't seem to be particularly fond of Rosellen, nor anyone else in the family for that matter, except possibly Birdie, and I wondered why she was so set on getting her released. Wondered too what made her think Howard could do it. I would have liked to have heard more. The scrap I did hear didn't tell me much. I didn't get a chance, though, as just then I saw the top of Alison's head as she climbed the stairs. I turned quickly and slipped into the room Birdie and I were sharing.

Later, after we were in our beds and the lights were out, Birdie said, "You don't think you can prove she didn't kill them, do you, Demary?"

"No, I don't," I said. There was no point in pretending otherwise. "But I will try. I'll do everything I can, but don't get your hopes up, Birdie."

"I won't," she said.

I heard her turn over in her bed and face the window. It was a long time before either of us went to sleep.

The next day, Friday, was what Birdie called "getting ready day." A day she claimed her mother had always made a fuss over when she and her brother were growing up. And she intended to make as big a fuss as possible over it today, the day before Rosellen's birthday. By noon a caterer from Seattle, hired by Birdie, had delivered and installed huge clusters of pink balloons all over the house and grounds—an act of faith on Birdie's part as June wasn't one of our more reliable months for sunny days. Happy Birthday streamers were everywhere, accompanied by florist's bouquets of multicolored flowers. The dining room table was covered with a lace cloth centered by a bowl of pink and white roses flanked by an array of pink candles in white ceramic holders.

Several packages with colorful ribbons were piled on the sideboard in front of the window.

"Mom always said just one day for something as important as a birthday wasn't enough," Birdie said happily, surveying the dining room table. "Chuck and I thought 'getting ready day' was every bit as much fun as the party the next day."

Rosellen seemed to think the same. Dressed in a frilly yellow dress, she went around burbling with smiles and laughter, her eyes sparkling with the fun of all the decorations.

Birdie watched her with fond eyes. "Isn't she pretty? Doesn't she look like a movie actress?" she asked me. "She was once."

"A movie actress?" I asked, startled.

"No, not really," Birdie said, smiling. "She was just a member of a local actors' guild or something, but when I was a kid I liked to pretend she was a movie actress. Mom said she was really good, didn't look like herself at all when she was acting in a play. She could change the way she walked and could even change her voice. A long time ago, before Grandpa died, we used to make up plays and things and everybody got to act in them. At Christmastime. Gran was always wonderful, and Howard, too. He could sound just like Grandpa. It was such fun." A lone tear slid down her cheek. She brushed it away angrily.

In the afternoon Birdie and I walked over to Jordan's house. I wanted to see how far away it was, how he kept it up, and to see if it gave me any ideas about the man himself. What little I'd seen of him the evening before had not left me with the impression of a heavy-drinking man. Neither did his house.

While the main house was encircled by well-kept lawns and heavy shrubbery, the cottage, as Birdie called it, was surrounded by beds of flowers, all in brilliant bloom and all carefully tended. The house had been painted within the last couple of years, the windows shone with fresh-washed cleanliness, and the small patio behind the house was not only swept, it had been hosed down. It was still wet in spots.

We didn't go inside. Jordan wasn't home. Birdie said he did his weekly shopping on Fridays. I did peek through the sliding glass door on the patio and saw a kitchen as well kept as the outside. All in all not the kind of place I would expect to be the home of a drinking man who had ended up in a drunk tank after a week of noisy partying.

That, of course, had happened twenty-some years ago. He could have seen the error of his ways long ago and taken some kind of cure, joined AA, or gotten religion. Any of which might be responsible for a change in the man. I wanted to talk to someone other than Birdie about him, though, and wondered if he had any longtime friends. People who had known him when Howard was alive.

"Not any that I know about," Birdie said when I asked her about his friends. "Actually, he acts like some kind of a hermit. Mom says he never has left the place much and never has anyone over to see him. She said Gran always said it was because he was wrapped up in his poetry, but Mom has never seen anything he wrote."

"What is he going to do when Junior sells the place?"

"The cottage is a separate tax lot. He says he isn't going to sell it." She stopped, thought a moment. "You know, it's kinda strange that he doesn't. I don't think Junior likes him very well; he always acts funny when he's around. Almost like he's afraid. But he never says anything to him. Jordan to Junior, I mean. Junior could sell the cottage if he wanted to; there isn't anything Jor-

dan could do about it, and then Junior wouldn't ever
have to see him again."

If I'd followed that correctly it was a bit strange. I had
noticed myself that the two men had seemed to stay
away from each other and didn't speak. Made me wonder if Jordan had some kind of hold over Junior. Not
necessarily anything sinister. It could be as simple as a
legal paper concerning the cottage. Something Howard
had given him years ago that gave him the right to live
in the cottage as long as he wished.

It was curious, though.

Chapter Nine

As soon as we got back to the house I stuck my cell phone in my pocket and went outside while Birdie was fussing with the packages for her grandmother. Once I was out of her sight I trotted down to the beach where I could be sure of reasonably good reception and called Martha. I had a long mental list of information I wanted her to look for and I didn't want Birdie to know what a couple of items were. I also needed the home phone number of Jake Allenby. I'd forgotten to bring my pocket notebook with me and knew his home telephone number was unlisted.

Jake and I were longtime friends. He had been a detective sergeant with the Seattle P.D. for nearly ten years but had quit Seattle some eight months previously to take a better-paying job with the Snohomish County Sheriff's Department. He wasn't entirely happy with his new position—it was a desk job—but Jake had a thirty-two-foot sailboat that cost big bucks to maintain. No police department pays the kind of money it takes to buy a boat that size, or to keep one in good shape. Jake, however, had won a chunk of the Washington State Lottery two years ago and had spent every penny of his winnings to buy the boat, which he owned outright, but, as he said, maintenance and moorage were eating him up alive. Hence his move to Snohomish and a bigger paycheck.

A break for me.

All the details of the Swallow murder investigation and subsequent court action were recorded somewhere in Snohomish County records. Some would be public record, which Martha would locate, but Jake might have access to the ones she couldn't get, such as the coroner's report. A coroner's report is considered a medical record and as such is not available to the public. And as it was all so long ago, I figured I'd be able to persuade him to dig it out and let me take a look at it. With Jake it was mostly a matter of how much work it would be for him to find them.

Not that I had any real hope of changing the status quo, but I was beginning to sense something off-center about the situation and it bothered me. Birdie had built me up to the family as an experienced private investigator, yet no one had asked me what I thought of the case, offered any information, or even spoken to me about Rosellen. Except for Junior, and that had been more of a warning off than anything else. In fact, the whole family seemed to be opposed to my investigating at all. No one except Ruth had mentioned the diary again after Junior had shown it to me. For all they knew I'd deciphered every bit of it and knew exactly where the missing money had gone, yet no one had asked a thing. There was something wrong with that.

The house was full of people but other than meeting— more or less—for dinner, none of them appeared to spend any time together. Nor did they have much to say to one another then. I had no idea if this was their normal behavior or if I was the inhibiting factor, but in either case it was like no family gathering I'd ever been around before.

In a way it was like being in a B&B where the guests were polite to one another but not particularly friendly.

My call caught Jake just as he was getting ready to leave for work, but he was, as usual, willing to help. He has a casual attitude toward departmental information anyway and in this case it was so far in the past it was ancient history as far as he was concerned.

"I've got to be out the door in about three minutes," he told me. "And I ought to tell you to do your own work, but you're in luck. I happened to see Wyndlow's file a couple of days ago. We've been transferring old files to computer disks, scanning them in, for the past several months. Dead boring mostly, but I got a kick out of his. The woman he was arrested with was old enough to be his grandmother and was a real terror. She hit the arresting officer with a geranium. I'll run you a copy of the report, and see what I can find on Swallow."

"Great, thanks Jake," I said, wondering if the geranium had been in a pot.

"No problem. I've got Sunday off. Or should have if some creep doesn't carve up a house full of his relatives. I'm taking the *Witch* out Sunday morning, just for the day—come on up and go, too. I'll have the stuff by then. I think Carol Ann and Frank are coming."

The *Blue Water Witch* was his boat, and a day sailing sounded wonderful. I told him I'd be there and we rang off.

Birdie's mother, Dorothy, and her brother, Chuck, arrived while Birdie and I were eating breakfast at the table in the kitchen the next morning. Dorothy was a plain-looking woman, with smooth salt-and-pepper gray hair, hazel eyes, and a wide mouth. Birdie looked nothing whatever like her but Chuck did, to the point of having prematurely gray hair and the same wide mouth. That feature seemed to run in the family. He was an accountant and worked for a firm in Olympia, was happily married, and had been for several years. No children.

Dorothy was a very "no-nonsense" kind of woman and she wasted no time asking me what foolishness I'd let Birdie talk me into.

"Oh, Mom," Birdie protested. "You make it sound like I twisted her arm."

"You probably did, one way or another," Dorothy said shortly, not sounding as if she was amused.

There was some truth in what she said. Not enough to bother me, though, and I wondered why it was bothering her. She knew me well enough to know I wouldn't be there if I didn't want to be.

"She asked me to look at the so-called diary," I said peaceably, deciding there was no sense in telling her any more than that and getting her more annoyed with Birdie than she already seemed to be. Especially since I didn't think I was going to accomplish much anyway.

"So-called? What do you mean, so-called?" she demanded. "I haven't seen it, but Junior definitely said it was Mother's diary."

I shrugged. "It doesn't look like a diary to me. And she said she'd never seen it before. Nor the desk." I hesitated. I might be making a mistake saying anything to anyone. After all, someone had killed Howard and that someone could well be in the house right now. "I looked in her room for a moment yesterday afternoon," I said finally. "And I've seen the desk. It doesn't look like the kind of thing Rosellen would use, nor does it either match or fit with her other furniture. And as far as I've been able to find out, nobody remembers ever seeing it in her room, either. Just makes me wonder."

Dorothy looked at me thoughtfully. "Don't go upsetting her, Demary. She's old now and not very strong. Be careful."

I nodded. Dorothy and I had always gotten along well but I had a feeling she could be ruthless if she thought the occasion important enough. She was fiercely protective of her mother, was a strong, athletic woman, and if Birdie had her facts right, had been at the house at least part of the time during the critical period twenty-two years ago.

The birthday party went off as planned and seemed to be enjoyed by everyone, especially the birthday girl. In a quiet moment when she was standing beside me she murmured that this was the first real birthday party she had ever had.

I left at daybreak the following morning, had a wonderful day aboard the *Blue Water Witch*, and arrived home late Sunday evening tired and sunburned.

Jake had given me a fat manila envelope full of reports and pictures he had copied, but I hadn't even opened it aboard the *Witch*. It had been too perfect a day for sailing to read about old crimes.

Chapter Ten

I had planned to be away for ten days so there was nothing pressing waiting for me Monday morning. I had three genealogy jobs I was working on in addition to the research on the *Kalakala* for Captain Nordan but I was waiting on information on all of them. So, in good conscience, I could do some work for Birdie.

When I got to the office I filled Martha in on everything I'd seen and heard at the Swallow place, commented on her outfit—an acid-green sheath that looked great on her tall, thin frame—and handed her a copy of the diary to look at. She's a lot better than I am at that kind of thing. She handed me a cup of coffee and I retired to my office to go through the file Jake had given me.

As Jake said, the reports on the arrest of Jordan Wyndlow were funny to visualize. He was thirty-two at the time. The lady with him first refused to say how old she was, then confessed to a wildly impossible thirty-nine. A check of her birth certificate showed her to be sixty-six, and according to the booking officer she looked every minute of her age. When arrested, both were dressed in skimpy swimsuits—hers a string bikini—while cavorting in a hot tub. They were drinking iced vodka out of cardboard milkshake containers, singing risqué lyrics to the tune of "Yankee Doodle"—loud enough to be heard several houses away—and eating Beluga caviar with their fingers.

Unfortunately, the first officer to answer the disturbance call was very young, and arresting a grandmother-aged, seminude, lady in these circumstances had not been covered in the police academy curriculum. Plus, he had nearly gotten himself drowned in the hot tub trying to drag the much larger Jordan out of the thing when Jordan had suddenly passed out.

The geranium had been only one of a dozen or more flowers the lady had pelted the poor young man with while he was struggling with Jordan. She had stuffed flowers down the front of his shirt and the back of his pants. He had no doubt taken a lot of razzing from fellow officers.

There was nothing funny about the rest of the reports.

The pathology summary explained why determining the time of death with any certainty had been impossible, and made my stomach lurch just reading it. Neither Howard nor Dian had actually died of the blows to their heads. They had died of asphyxia, with evidence of contributing hyperthermia. Both had been alive when put into the freezer. The examiner was sure both had been unconscious and, as the freezer had not been locked, or even latched, and could easily have been pushed open, it was unlikely that they had ever come out of it enough to know where they were. A truly horrifying crime.

Howard had been a large man weighing two hundred and twelve pounds. Dian, at five foot seven, weighed one hundred and fifty-two. Nothing in any of the notes or reports suggested how four-foot-eleven, ninety-pound Rosellen got them into the freezer, a twenty-seven-cubic-foot commercial chest variety that stood forty-three inches high.

There was no trace in the shed of any kind of block and tackle, pulley, hoist, or any other contrivance that could have helped her get them into the thing, and no one interviewed had ever seen anything like that about the place. Nor was there any evidence of their being dragged or pulled across the floor.

Martha came in and put some papers on my desk just as I finished that file. I handed it to her wordlessly.

She read it through, shuddering as she got to the end, and handed it back. "I'm glad this took place twenty-two years ago," she said, grimacing. "We can at least hope whoever did it has either learned the error of his ways and is now a model citizen, or has moved somewhere else. Preferably to another continent."

"Anything else strike you about it?"

"No, unless you mean the impossibility of Rosellen doing it herself. She could have had help, though, or she could have been a lot stronger than her size indicates."

"How about the attached test results?"

She picked up the file again and checked the contents register stapled to the inside of the front cover. "There aren't any other than the standard blood typing," she said, surprised. "I wonder why not? They surely did some, at least blood alcohol level."

"If they did they weren't included in the report."

"Maybe Jake just didn't put . . . No, that isn't right. Everything they did should be on the register even if he didn't send a copy. But . . ." She skimmed through the attached sheets again. "This wasn't done by a lab. It was done by an M.D."

"M-m-huh. He was probably the coroner. The county may not have had a regular coroner at the time. Lots of places didn't back then. A local doctor usually did the honors. But it is still odd."

She frowned at me. "Hold on a minute. Let me go get Howard's death certificate. I phoned and had it faxed from Olympia after you called."

She went out and came back in a moment waving a fax. "I thought I remembered. Look. Cause of death: Severe blunt trauma to the right occipital."

"Now that is strange," I said thoughtfully. "Very strange."

"Very, and so is that," she said, nodding at the papers she had brought in earlier. "I got a condensed copy of the competency hearing, actually looks like a press hand-out, and it is more than strange. No psychiatric report referred to, nor any psychiatrist present. How can you have a competency hearing without a psychiatrist having some say in the matter? Who decided, and on what grounds? Did Birdie say? After all, this was just twenty-some years ago, not back in the dark ages."

"As far as she seems to know, simply on the basis of Rosellen's behavior, which according to Birdie was more hysterical than anything else, and certainly normal under the circumstances."

Martha stared at me. "Why is she asking you to investigate the murder now? Why just now? Has something happened recently? Other than finding that so-called diary, which, incidentally, doesn't look like any kind of a diary to me."

I shook my head. "Nothing that I know of. Except Junior wants to sell the house."

"Birdie has known you for years. Knows what you do. Why did she wait until now to ask you to look into the murder?"

"What are you getting at?"

"The only thing different is the sale of the house. Maybe that means something. She was there during the critical time; you said so. Young teenager, money missing. Maybe . . ."

"Oh, come on, Martha. Birdie? Don't be silly."

She made a wry face. "H-m-m. You're probably right. Anyway, I've got work to do. I've got a stack of briefs to do for Anna Carmine."

She went back out, frowning at my new wall hanging as she went. She wasn't sure she liked it. It was a traditional Oriental design in indigo blue and white with Japanese Sashiko quilting. I wasn't sure about it myself, and had to admit it didn't go well in a room with tangerine-colored chairs. Much as I liked the chairs' bright color, maybe I'd have to replace them.

I'm Martha's primary employer but I can't begin to pay her what she's worth, so she functions as receptionist for all the tenants of the building and is paid accordingly by them also. And as long as it doesn't interfere with anything I want her to do, she also does some word processing for Anna Carmine, our resident attorney, when she doesn't have a clerk. Her last law clerk, Jodie Dunham, was presently clerking for the district attorney. Which reminded me I wanted to ask Anna about the firm Howard had been working for at the time of the murders, plus what she might know, if anything, about the judge. Jake had told me he was still on the bench.

I booted up my PC and started keyboarding in everything I'd seen or heard regarding the Swallow case and the people I'd met over the weekend. I didn't try to make any sense of it, not yet. I think better looking at a computer screen and once it was all there in front of me I could start sorting. I could also pick out names. People that might have something interesting to say in a face-to-face interview. Not family members, but people such as that young arresting officer, or the bank teller who claimed to have spoken to Howard after he was supposedly already dead. Another one I'd like to locate was the housekeeper Birdie had mentioned, and the detective in charge of the case. His name was on several reports—Leon Kieski—but as far as I could tell he had never signed off on the investigation. Theoretically, it was still open.

There was something extremely odd about the whole case. Nothing matched.

Chapter Eleven

Martha stuck her head in my door a few minutes before twelve to tell me she was going to lunch with Charles, her husband who was a professor at the U of W, and probably wouldn't be back until after three. If she came back at all.

"They serve a slap-up lunch but by the time I sit through listening to them gossip about all their friends who aren't there I'll likely have a thundering headache," she said, making a sour face.

I'd planned to be gone all week so she had scheduled several things she wouldn't have bothered with if I'd been there. This was a faculty lunch, which she avoided as a rule, but it was politic to attend occasionally.

She said she'd lock up before she left. Four other businesses shared the premises with me but they all had their own separate entrances on the parking lot back of the building as well as access through the reception area facing 45th Street. Martha's desk with computer, fax, copier, and so forth could be sealed off by lowering, and locking, a fancy grill.

I meant to skip lunch but it was such a beautiful day I changed my mind and decided to walk up to my favorite restaurant, Julia's on 44th and Wallingford. When I turned the corner in front of the old Wallingford school I saw my teenage pal Joey Winters across the street with a girl about his own age. I didn't hail him. Teenagers being as they are I wasn't sure he'd want to acknowledge knowing me but I should have known better. Joey is his own man. He came bounding across the street, against the light, calling to me to wait up.

He dodged between two cars that were stopped for the light, dragging his friend along beside him. She was a beautiful little thing with curly black hair cut in a boyish crop, bright blue eyes, and a slender figure.

He came to a stop in front of me and introduced the girl immediately. "Demary, this is my friend Janay Hollie. Janay, Demary Jones. She's the detective I work with that I told you about."

I swallowed that without a visible gulp. His idea of working with me wasn't the same as mine. In fact, I did my best to keep him away from any detecting I was doing. But Joey is a born snoop and the kind of kid who not only knows everybody in the entire neighborhood, he knows everything going on in the neighborhood as well. Which he immediately proved.

"Have you made any progress yet with the Swallow problem?" he asked blandly.

I did gulp on that one. I hadn't been home twenty-four hours and the Swallow problem, as he called it, was definitely not a neighborhood affair. The problem, such as it was, hadn't even taken place in the same county. How in the world had he gotten wind of it?

He told me.

"Buddy Swallow lives next door to Janay," he said.

"Or at least his mother does and he's staying with her for a couple of weeks. His parents split. He told me all about the dumb stunt he pulled with the doll. Kid hasn't got good sense. His dad makes him dress like a nerd, so no wonder. He does better when he's with his mother for a while."

I found this commentary interesting in light of Joey's normal attire. He was slightly more conventionally dressed today, inasmuch as his jeans were almost new, and his T-shirt reasonably whole with an only mildly bizarre cartoon on the front of it. Or at least I thought it was mild by Joey standards. I may not have understood it.

"I'm very pleased to meet you," Janay said in a soft voice. "I've always lived next door to Mrs. Swallow's family. Her mother and father lived there before. She used to baby-sit me when I was little; now I baby-sit little Ellen sometimes. We're on our way to talk to her."

"To Ellen? What in the world for?" I asked, trying not to sound alarmed.

"Ellen wouldn't talk to Joey, but she will to me," Janay said composedly. "I'll find out if she knows anything, but we have to hurry. Mrs. Swallow is taking them to the zoo this afternoon."

With that the two of them said good-bye and took off running before I could get my wits together. Actually I was too stunned to speak. Having Joey snoop was hair-raising enough. Involving his pretty little girlfriend was enough to scare me rigid. The last friend he involved in his snooping ended up with all his hair shaved off.

What in the world did the two kids think eight-year-old Ellen could possibly know anyway? And for all the proof I had one way or the other, Ruth could be the murderer. She had only been eighteen at the time and according to Birdie hardly knew Junior then, or anyone else in the family, but that was only Birdie's version. Many an eighteen-year-old had committed murder and for all kinds of reasons. She could even have been in love with the senior Howard. Eighteen-year-old girls have done stranger things than fall in love with an older man.

Somehow I was going to have to persuade Joey to keep out of this one even if it was ancient history.

I had a hummus roll-up for lunch. Like everything else on Julia's menu, it was delicious. A whole-wheat tortilla filled with hummus, sprouts, tomatoes, cucumber, and avocado. I washed it down with a glass of raspberry tea.

I didn't have anything I had to do so when I finished eating I spent a half hour in the Second Story Bookstore across the street in the Wallingford Mall. It was after two before I got back to the office. Martha was still out but I found I had a message from Sam on the answering machine asking me to call him.

Sam Morgan is a lieutenant in the Seattle P.D. homicide division. He and I go back a long way. He's a good-looking guy, kind of a combination Robert Redford/Paul Newman but with dark hair and dimples. We have an on-again/off-again relationship. We almost got married once but that idea came to an abrupt halt when we had one of our frequent disagreements over Sam trying to tell me what to do. We aren't exactly friends—we're more than that, usually—but we aren't in love with each other.

"How did you know I was here?" I asked when he answered the phone. I'd told him I was going to Alaska.

"I saw Carol Ann this morning. She told me you all had been boating yesterday," he said, not sounding pleased.

I mentally ground my teeth. I have enough trouble getting along with Sam without Carol Ann sticking her two cents' worth in. She is Seattle P.D. also and dearly loves to get under Sam's skin by telling him when I've been somewhere with Jake Allenby. She has a primitive sense of humor. Although why Sam thinks he has any right to monitor my activities I'll never know.

"What happened to your Alaska trip?" he asked.

I told him, and for once he didn't jump all over me for interfering in police business. In fact, he even offered to help if there was anything he could do. That left me practically speechless. He no doubt felt that deciphering an old diary was a safe project for me. I didn't tell him a murder went along with it. What he didn't know he couldn't yell at me about.

"How about having dinner?" he asked. "I'll take you to that salmon place you like."

"Why don't I fix something instead?" I asked. I didn't feel like going anywhere. "Come over about six and I'll make some stir-fry. I bought a bunch of fresh stuff at an open-air market on the way home yesterday."

"Sounds good," he said agreeably. "I'll bring the wine."

We chatted for a few minutes longer and then rang off.

I went back to work reading the files Jake had given me. In fact, I read and reread them several times without getting any clearer picture of the investigation. I finally made up a list of people I wanted to talk to, left a note for Martha asking her to see if she could locate them, and took off for home.

I have a perfectly wonderful house. My great-aunt left it to me in her will, along with a horrendous mortgage that I've gradually whittled down to manageable size.

It's three stories high, with carved railings around the porches, elaborate window frames, scalloped and diamond-shaped shingles, and an ornate front door. The fancy door is the result of a counterfeiter trying to blow up the place. He was also responsible for the new paint job, a gleaming white that more than ever makes the place look like a Victorian wedding cake.

The house has a few disadvantages, such as only one bathroom and a kitchen on the second floor the size of a skating rink. There is a dining room but I set the dishes for dinner in the corner of the kitchen on the small table in front of the window that overlooks the backyard. I like the table there so I can look out at the little fish pond in the center that I surround with pots of bright red geraniums. The yard itself is mostly tile, with a few ornamental trees in big pottery tubs. Gardening is definitely not my thing. Not only do I hate grubbing around in the dirt, I have long ago come to the conclusion that gardening is a masochistic endeavor at best. If the slugs don't defeat you the weather will.

Sam got there a few minutes before six and I surprised both of us by giving him a welcoming hug and kiss.

We had a great evening, never once mentioning what I was beginning to think of by Joey's appellation as "the Swallow problem."

Chapter Twelve

It was raining the next morning when I woke up. A soft, misty rain that was more like a heavy fog than real rain. June is an uncertain month when it comes to the weather in the Northwest. It was a jeans kind of day but too warm for a sweater so I settled for an expensive designer sweatshirt with a multicolored flower scene appliqued on the front of it. I'd bought it in one of the weak moments that come over me when I go to one of the Bon Marche's big sales.

I didn't linger over my breakfast of coffee and a croissant, and the first thing I did when I got to the office was to go along to Anna Carmine's office. I knew she had to be in court by ten—she was working on an insurance fraud case—and I wanted to catch her before she left.

"Have you got a minute to talk?" I asked when she answered my knock with an impatient, "Come on in, the door isn't locked."

"I need some information about lawyers," I said, eyeing her latest courtroom outfit. No severely tailored gray

68

suits for Anna. She had on flame-colored linen slacks with a long, unstructured jacket in a slightly lighter color over an orange silk blouse. With her bony five-foot-five figure, black hair cut in its short flip style, and snapping black eyes, she looked stunning.

"What kind of information?" she asked, stuffing papers into her briefcase. "Fifty percent of the lawyers I know never should have passed the bar. The rest aren't too bad if you can afford a good one."

"Like you."

"Right." She grinned. "What do you need, Demary?"

I laughed. "I want to know how I can find out about a law firm that was active in Everett twenty some years ago."

"Do you know the firm name, or the names of the partners?"

"Wellman, Bowers and Cranmer is what's on some of the court records. Howard Swallow IV was one of the associates at the time. It doesn't appear to be in business any more. Or it isn't in the phone book, anyway."

"Oh. The Swallow murder. Birdie Swallow's grandfather. Martha was telling me about the case last week. Friday. I don't know anything about the firm myself—I was still in law school when it happened—but I do know someone who might."

"Who?"

"Professor Bacon. James Bacon. He's retired now but he was teaching at the time of the murder. It wasn't really big news, not in all the papers anyway, but if I'm not mistaken I think I remember him saying that one of the firm partners had been his student for a couple of years."

"Will he talk to me?"

"What do you want to know about them?"

"Simply if they were considered a top-of-the-line firm, or just another bunch of lawyers. It looks to me as if they mishandled the competency hearing. Plus I'd like to know about the judge, too."

"I doubt if he'd respond to those sort of questions. In fact I'm pretty sure he wouldn't. As far as telling you anything negative about them, anyway. But he might tell me. I'll call him, but I won't have time until this afternoon." She glanced at her watch. "And if I don't get a move on I'll be late to court. I'll let you know."

She started out and then turned back, one hand on the door. "You say you have some of the court records?"

"Just those Jake got for me. I don't think they are complete by any means."

"Well, have Martha see what she can find on the trust. It should be public record. From what she told me Friday I'm wondering how legal sharing out any of the sale of the house proceeds might be. Didn't you tell Martha they intended to divide some of it among the three families?"

"That was the impression I got."

"Depends on what the trust conditions are, but I doubt if Howard can do that without the court's consent."

With that, she strode off down the hall leaving me to lock up after her.

Martha had just come in and was sorting the morning's mail when I went back to my own office.

"This looks like the stuff you've been waiting for on the La Rocques," she said, handing me a fat manila envelope with a Strasbourg, France postmark.

I opened the envelope eagerly. Researching the La Rocque family tree had been interesting. Mrs. Davis, born Maria La Rocque, had hired me. She was quite proud of what she knew of the family history and thought a family tree, done up in book form with pictures, would be a really different thing to give to her niece, her brother's daughter, for a wedding gift.

Mrs. Davis's grandfather, Henri La Rocque, had been a Resistance fighter in France during the second world war. He had apparently been quite a hero, as he had been decorated by both the British and the French. De Gaulle had personally pinned the Legion of Honor medal on his chest. He had been wounded during the Normandy landings and had been evacuated to London on one of the hospital ships where he met, and married, Lieutenant Dorothy Thomas, an American army nurse. They spent several years in London and in Paris but came to the States when Dorothy became pregnant with Mrs. Davis's father. The next forty years were uneventful as far as the family history in this country was concerned, but when I began to trace Henri back a few generations I found some material Mrs. Davis wasn't expecting. Henri's great-grandfather had come from Alsace-Lorraine where a number of distant relatives still lived. I had made contact with one of this group who told me the family was well known in the region and could be traced, loosely, back to the time of Charlemagne when the territory had still been part of the Holy Roman Empire.

The manila envelope held copies of all his documentation. This was the kind of discovery that makes genealogy such fun, and Mrs. Davis was going to be delighted.

I worked on the La Rocque information until after lunchtime when Martha came in with some interesting material on the Swallow estate trust. Interesting because it didn't exist. Or at least it had never been legally filed anywhere, and there was no court record of it at any time.

Martha has developed a network of what she calls co-snoops that makes the CIA look like a bunch of kids playing I Spy in the backyard. She talks to these people, mostly women, via chat rooms, e-mail, and bulletin boards. They help her gather all kinds of data. Some of her correspondents even seem to get a charge out of digging up the information she wants by personally looking through old newspaper files, public records, and/or anything else they can think of, including listening to back-fence gossip.

Gossip, or at least the memory of a conversation, had paid off this time. The mother of one of her co-snoops' friends had been part of the building maintenance crew the year of the murder and was in and out of the courthouse every day. She remembered the so-called competency hearing very distinctly because, according to her, it had been a complete farce with everybody screaming and/or crying and had ended in a closed session in the judge's chambers. Gossip around the courthouse in the days that followed was that whatever had been decided in there had not been recorded in the court calendar, nor anywhere else.

If true, this could have been a complete misuse of the court's powers. Rosellen's civil rights had been ignored and she had not only been illegally incarcerated all these years, everything she owned had been taken from her. Stolen.

As it turned out Martha's informant was only half right. The recording hadn't been done that day, nor even that week, as Martha found out for herself later in the day. She came in looking upset, unusual for her, and slapped a computer printout on the desk in front of me.

"Take a look at this, Demary. It may not be Rosellen but somebody in that Swallow bunch is definitely round the twist."

A record of the court's proceedings had been duly filed but not until ten days after the fact. Like most legal documents they were hard to decipher and, to me, seemed to be incomplete. The more important fact, however, was that they had been filed the same day Rosellen had been admitted *on her own signature* to the Windsor House for psychiatric care.

Chapter Thirteen

"What do you suppose put the frighteners on her? Made her willing to go to Windsor rather than push the system to prove her innocence?" Martha asked.

"Junior must have threatened her with something. But what?" I wondered aloud, scowling at the admittance form Martha had managed to get a hold of. I had no intention of asking her how she'd done it. Her methods weren't always what they should be.

"I'd say the thought of at least twenty years of hard time might do it," she said sourly. "But why do you say threaten?"

"Because he strikes me as the kind who would threaten. But that wasn't what I meant. He couldn't have."

"If you mean sons don't do that kind of thing to their mothers, think again. It's been done before, and for far less lolly than seems to be involved here."

"No. I mean there wasn't enough evidence of her guilt to convict. All they had was her fingerprints on the pipe and they were easily explained away. And that court

74

stuff was really strange. Sounds almost as if Junior and the judge came to a private agreement to put her away."

We were still kicking the legality of that idea around five minutes later when there was a knock on the door and Joey's voice called, "Demary? Demary? Are you in there?"

Martha got up and opened the door to admit Joey and his pretty girlfriend Janay. Janay's eyes were wide with what looked like fright and even Joey, normally imperturbable, appeared shaken. As it turned out, however, he was just angry, with, of all people, Sam Morgan.

"Your cop friend is a no-good . . ." He stopped, took a deep breath, and started again. "Your cop friend doesn't have good sense," he said. "He wanted to know what we were doing there and then asked Janay where she was last night, when she went to bed, what she'd heard. She never even talked to a cop before. He scared her."

"Joey told him if he didn't leave me alone he was going to call CPS, or my mother," Janay said in a pleased voice.

Both Martha and I stared at them, bewildered.

"CPS? Child Protective Services?" I asked, totally confused. "You told Sam you were going to call . . . What in the world for? Why was he asking her anything? Where were you, Joey?"

"At Mrs. Swallow's house. Somebody stabbed her to death," he said bluntly.

Janay's eyes got even bigger. She looked like a little owl. I was about to tell Joey he was the one who was scaring her when what he'd said sunk in.

"What? What did you say?" I gasped. " "Mrs. Swallow, Ruth Swallow, was murdered? Somebody stabbed . . . When?"

"Sometime last night. The kids found her this morning. Must have scared them half to death. Buddy at least had sense enough to call his dad. One of the neighbors said your friend Birdie took them away later. Good thing Morgan didn't talk to them; that would have finished them for sure," he said, jabbing his fists in the air like a prize fighter.

Martha took Janay's arm and sat her down in one of the tangerine-colored chairs. I had a feeling Janay wasn't really all that upset. Sam may have asked her a few questions but he hadn't stayed a lieutenant for all these years by being stupid. He would not have been rough with Janay. Joey was just being macho.

"All right, calm down," I told him. "Start at the beginning and tell me what happened. The last time I saw you, yesterday afternoon, you were on your way over to Mrs. Swallow's house to see Ellen and Buddy. Did you see them?"

"No, they had already left for the zoo. When Janay called me this morning and told me about all the cops being there I went over to see what was going on. I went through the Jackson yard on Corliss, across the alley to Jimmy Carmichael's house, and then through his backyard to Janay's. Janay and Mrs. Swallow live on Bagley. That way the cops didn't see me. We went upstairs to where I could see out the window what was going on."

I had a fleeting thought that someday Joey was going to be a really great detective. He had all the right instincts.

"I could see the scene-of-the-crime boys and the evidence recorder and all the rest of them milling around but I couldn't hear anything so we decided to go out in the backyard where we could listen to what they were saying."

"Where was you mother?" I asked Janay, wondering why she hadn't stopped them from getting into trouble.

"At work. Both she and my dad work the early shift at Boeing. They used to take me out to my aunt's house but they said I was old enough to be on my own some this summer. I'm almost fourteen. I'm going to a girls' camp in Wyoming in a couple of weeks."

I made myself a mental note to have a word with her later, in private.

Joey gave one of his exasperated sighs, showing off for his little friend. "You want to hear the rest of this?" he asked.

"I'm listening," I said, watching Martha struggle to keep a straight face.

"We watched through the bushes and waited until no one was looking and then I climbed the big maple tree at the side of the Swallow house. Half of it hangs over Janay's yard and once I was up high enough so nobody could see me through the leaves I just scooted out on one of the big branches and I could hear everything."

Martha rolled her eyes at me. "Proper little peeper, you are," she told Joey. "Wonder Morgan didn't sort you out good."

"Ha. He never knew I was up there. So when I heard all I wanted I climbed down. They had that yellow 'do not cross' tape in the front of the house but nothing around the back so we went through the bushes and were in the backyard when Morgan saw us out of the kitchen window and yelled at us. Wanted to know what we were doing there. Then he came out and started asking questions."

"He had a perfect right to ask questions," I said

sternly. Joey can get carried away sometimes. "You knew better than to be in that yard. What happened after that?"

"He sent us home and told us to mind our own business. Which didn't do him any darn good," Joey said, pleased with himself. "We came straight up here."

Finally, reluctantly, I asked Joey to tell me what he'd learned. Truth was, I really didn't want to know. What kind of a world were we living in when some kind of a nut-case could kill a nice woman like Ruth in her own home? And this sort of thing happened all too frequently. It was just a wonder that whoever had done it hadn't killed the children, too.

"I heard one of the men say whoever did it came through the laundry room window, made his way upstairs, and stabbed her with a knife from the kitchen."

"She was in her bedroom?" Alarm bells jangled in my head.

"In bed, asleep. Never knew a thing is what one of the cops said."

I caught my breath in surprise. If Joey had heard right it hadn't been the random violence I'd thought. It had been a premeditated murder. And possibly done by the same person who had killed Howard so long ago. But why? What had happened to make him, or her, kill again?

Had Ruth said or done something over the weekend that frightened the killer? She hadn't even been around when Howard was stuffed in the freezer. What could she possibly know that was a danger to anyone at this late date?

This didn't make any more sense than the rest of the Swallow problem. If something had happened over the weekend, why hadn't the killer done his killing then when Ruth was easily available? No, it had to be random violence.

Martha disagreed when I voiced the thought to her after the kids left to go to Joey's house where his mother was fixing them lunch.

"No, whoever he is, he's too fly for that. If he'd offed her then, at the house, it would have been too obvious. This way you can't be sure who did it, or why."

Chapter Fourteen

I thought about calling Sam but decided, no, I wasn't going to get involved in the investigation of Ruth's death. The homicide department—as Sam had told me innumerable times—was perfectly capable of solving its cases without any help from me.

I'd stick to trying to decipher the diary, and to maybe getting a handle on Rosellen's situation at the same time. Why and how she was placed in Windsor House was the biggest question in my mind, not whether she had killed her husband, or not.

Good thing I didn't bet any money on the thought, though, because five minutes later I was right in the middle of it. Sam called and demanded to know why Ruth had called me last night.

"She didn't," I said, crossly, feeling my good intentions dribbling off down the drain. "What makes you think she did?"

"The last number on her redial is yours," he said, still sounding like he was interrogating a serial killer. "So what did she have to say?"

"I said I didn't talk to her," I snapped. "You came over for dinner, remember? No one called and you didn't leave until late. So . . . ?" This didn't sound like it was going to be one of our better days. A murder that I had any connection to at all always made Sam cranky.

"Oh, yes." He didn't say anything for a moment, didn't apologize either, then asked in a more normal tone, "Did you check your messages this morning?"

"Yes. She didn't leave a message. Any idea what time she called? It must have been late. Or I suppose she could have called before I got home."

"Any idea why she'd call at all?"

"No." I thought for a bit. She had been pleasant but certainly nothing more than that the few times I'd seen her. "No, I only spoke to her a couple of times. On Thursday. Maybe she wasn't the one who phoned. Joey said Birdie took the two children away; maybe she was there last night and was the one who called." I thought a moment. "No, that can't be right. She would have left a message."

"Maybe." Someone in his office said something to him and he put his hand over the mouthpiece for a moment. "Anyway, I want to talk to you about her—Mrs. Swallow," he said finally, returning. "I'll be out there later. And in the meantime, you talk to that kid. Keep him out of my hair."

That irked me. "What do you mean, talk to him? He wasn't the only kid standing around watching what was going on this morning." That was a guess but I knew I was right. Every boy in the neighborhood would have been there taking it all in. Certainly Jimmy Carmichael would have been. He was a worse snoop than Joey.

Sam made a noncommittal noise and hung up. I slammed my long-suffering phone onto its base and turned to my computer to bring up my files on the Swallow case. I don't keyboard in absolutely everything I see or hear when I'm working on a case, but even on the small things I put in enough to remind me of the incident whether I think it's important or not. One of the things I'd noted was the scrap of conversation I'd overheard in the hall Thursday night between Ruth and Junior. I'd forgotten about it until I saw it on the screen.

When I'd spoken to Ruth just before we went down to the beach that evening, she told me she was leaving after dinner and wouldn't be back until Sunday morning to pick up the two children. That had been around six. It had been close to eleven when I heard her from the hall. I'd neither seen nor heard her at any time in between. None of which was either illicit or even too strange—she could have changed her mind or simply been elsewhere in the house—but it did raise questions in my mind. Particularly so now, of course.

It also gave Junior a possible motive for murder.

"No, I think he's out of it," Sam told me late that afternoon when he came to the office. "He was in Bellingham from ten yesterday morning until six-thirty this morning. A dozen witnesses including the judge he was arguing a case in front of can testify to his whereabouts until one o'clock last night when he checked into his hotel room. He, the assistant DA, and three other attorneys went up to Vancouver, B.C., for dinner after they got out of court. He could have made it down here and back by the time he checked out again at six-thirty this morning, but it would have been a tight fit. We will check his story, though."

I frowned at him. "You don't think it was just a random thing, do you?"

"No, I don't, but I can't be sure either. Entry was through the laundry room window; it was apparently unlocked. The room is also the pantry—several cans and a container of sugar were knocked over onto the floor and some of the sugar was tracked through the kitchen and into the hall."

"Footprints?"

"Not enough to make out the size or kind of shoe, but there were traces, grains, in the upstairs hall and in the bedroom. The knife was on the floor next to the bed. It came from a set that was in one of those knife-holder things that was sitting on the end of the counter beside the pantry door. The perp may have come equipped with something else and simply grabbed the knife for reasons of his own, or may have known the knives were there. No way of telling."

"What else?"

"Nothing so far. The lab boys are going over everything with a fine-tooth comb but I don't think they are going to find much. She was lying on her back and the first slash went through the blanket and sheet covering her, so the blood was all contained. No spurts to catch the perp's clothes or shoes."

"No fingerprints?"

He shook his head, sighing. "They all watch too darn much television. He was wearing gloves and took them with him when he left, we think through the back door. There were grains of sugar on the back porch."

"You said 'he.' Could it have been a woman?"

"Easy. She was asleep and it doesn't look like she ever woke up at all. Other than the hump her body made, the bed was perfectly smooth. No sign of any disturbance. Nothing in the room is upset, either."

"It doesn't sound random," I said, feeling a chill run

down my spine. "How about the rest of the house? Anything trashed? Missing?"

"Nothing. At least not as far as we can tell. Her mother is supposed to check out her jewelry and any valuables she had tomorrow morning but nothing in the house appears to be displaced. In fact, if we believe the sugar trail, he went directly to her room and out again without even going into any other room."

"*If* you believe the sugar trail?"

"It could have been faked."

"Why?"

He shook his head. "Too soon to guess."

"If it wasn't random then someone had a motive. Who? I don't know enough about her to even make a guess."

"You know more than I do, so let's talk about the people you met at the Swallow place," he said, sounding official again.

I frowned at him. I didn't like his tone to start with but mainly I didn't see any connection. I'd been thinking about it, hard, ever since Joey had told me about her death, and I couldn't think of any reason one of the Swallows would want to kill her. She was no longer married into the family; she and Junior seemed to have an amiable relationship, and I couldn't see her murder having its roots way back in the other killing, either. She had barely known the family then. All of which I relayed to Sam.

He shrugged. "You're probably right but all of them will have to be checked out and it will be easier if I know something about them."

I thought a moment. "Well, you've met Birdie. She's about as likely to kill anyone as I am to sign up for a trip to the moon. Dorothy, Birdie's mother, can be tough about things but I sincerely doubt her ability to stab Ruth. She's too levelheaded and doesn't have a motive anyway." I stopped, my mind switching rapidly through all the Swallows, and Jordan Wyndlow. "What possible motive do any of them have?" I asked.

"I don't have any idea yet. At the moment, none that I know of, but I still want to have your impressions of them."

I decided that was a backhanded compliment and went on a bit more cordially. "I didn't like either of the Davises. Allison Davis is Birdie's aunt. Both she and her husband, George, struck me as thinking they were somehow better than anyone else. Jordan Wyndlow, and I'm not sure of the relationship there, he's actually Rosellen Swallow's kin, is a big guy and would be physically capable of the murder, but again, what possible motive could he have?" I thought a moment. "He came across to me as being more gentle than violent in any way."

"People aren't always what they seem," he said grimly. "Jordan has been arrested three times on assault charges. They were all a long time ago and the cases were all dismissed, but he was definitely guilty. The women simply wouldn't press charges."

That certainly gave me a new slant on things. Maybe Birdie had been right to be afraid of him.

Chapter Fifteen

Before he left Sam told me at least three times to keep my nose out of Ruth's murder investigation, and for once I was truthful in telling him I'd obey him to the letter. He didn't believe me but that was his problem. I truly did not want anything to do with the case and told Birdie so in no uncertain terms when she called not five minutes after he went out the door and wanted me to find the killer.

"Birdie, you must be off your nut," I said, none too gently. "You absolutely can not keep on thinking I'm a PI. I'm not!"

"But you've solved lots of murders," she wailed. "I know you have."

"Yes, I have helped solve a couple of cases, but they weren't anything like this. The very thought of tangling with whoever did this scares the pudding out of me. And it should scare you too. Whatever is the matter with you, girl?" I was beginning to wonder if Birdie was all right in the head. Maybe Rosellen wasn't the only one in the family that wasn't firing on all eight cylinders.

"But you're already trying to solve Grandpa's murder. You can easily—"

"No, I can't," I said firmly. "So just forget it, Birdie. I am trying to figure out the diary and I'm looking into the rest of what happened twenty years ago, but that's it. You hear me?"

Martha was standing in the doorway when I hung up. "What's got up your nose about Ruth's death?" she asked. "You sound, uh . . ."

"Nervous? Jittery? I am, and I don't know why. I was thoroughly frightened when I found that dead man in the backyard of Sherry's apartment while I was staying there, but nothing like this. I'm not actually scared but for some reason I just don't want anything to do with Ruth's death. There's an almost eerie feeling to the killing. And with the two kids right in the next room, it gives me the creepy crawlies. It was so deliberate, so . . . oh, I don't know, so businesslike, so efficient somehow. Nothing in the house was disturbed, not even her bedding. Somebody simply came in, stabbed her, and walked out."

She looked at me thoughtfully. "Yes, it was, uh, is, different," she said finally.

"Even the sugar doesn't ring true. It's as if the killer purposefully left a trail, making sure the cops knew what he'd come for. Almost like he was challenging Sam, saying, catch me if you can."

I hesitated and then went on. "I know Birdie is my friend and I'd like to do what she wants, but I didn't know Ruth. I met her the one time. I wouldn't even know where to start." I sounded defensive even to myself but Martha didn't argue. In fact, she agreed with Sam—for once.

"I think you're right," she said sharply. "No sense to

go haring off trying to solve a crime that doesn't have anything to do with you. Plus, you're not getting paid for it."

I couldn't help smiling. The bottom line, what I'm getting paid for my efforts, is inevitably one of Martha's prime criteria.

We locked up a few minutes later and I went home to straighten up the mess I'd made of my bedroom when I'd come home from Sunday's sailing. I'd left my open suitcase on the floor, plus some of my clothes draped over the chair, and the end of my bed. Wednesday was Nora's day to clean and I didn't dare leave my room in such a mess. I had inherited Nora along with the house. That is, she had been working for my aunt when she died and had agreed to stay on and give me a try. We were still on that basis. She keeps my house sparkling from top to bottom but has no patience with clothes left lying around or dirty dishes left in the sink. Not that she doesn't take care of them—she does, sometimes—but she is also quite capable of throwing any clothes left on the floor into the trash. She had done so once and left on the floor into the trash. She had done so once and left me an astringent note regarding my slovenly habits.

She is not by any stretch of the imagination the old family retainer type. She is younger than I am, dresses better, and drives a Porsche.

I took some time getting dressed the next morning. Martha had located Leon Kieski, the detective who had been in charge of the Swallow murder case. He was retired and lived alone in a small house in Everett. He'd been fifty-one at the time of Howard's death. Martha had made an appointment for me to see him without any problem. He'd been perfectly willing to talk to me, which was a surprise. I'd had the feeling that no one connected with the case wanted to talk about it, although I didn't know what had given me the idea. At any rate he said he'd be glad to see me as long as I wasn't, in his words, "One of them hard-boiled female private eyes." So although I wasn't about to wear ruffled gingham, I thought a dress might be better than jeans and a Seahawk sweatshirt. I settled finally on a two-piece Liz Claiborne outfit in a pale green cotton check with pink satin trim that looks surprisingly good with my auburn hair.

Joey was leaning against the hood of the Toyota when I went out. I don't have a garage—it fell down before my aunt died—and I've never been able to persuade the city to give me a permit to build another. They say the lot is too narrow to put the garage where I want it. I say there was a garage there to start with and the lot certainly didn't shrink, but so far that reasoning hasn't done me any good.

" 'Morning, Demary," he said cheerfully, flashing his braces at me. "You going up around Everett this morning?"

"M-m-huh," I said, wondering if Joey had added mind-reading to his many talents. "Do you want to go?"

"Can't," he said regretfully. "My cell phone is wacked."

Joey seems to be on his own a lot, free to come and go as he pleases, but the truth is his mother always knows exactly where he is. His father is an airline pilot and is gone a lot. I used to think the reason he stayed in such constant touch with her was to reassure her about himself but I've come to realize it's the other way around. He stays in contact to make sure she is okay.

"You can use mine," I said, taking it out of my shoulder bag and handing it to him. "I'd just as soon have company on the drive."

"All right!" He quickly punched in the number and after a brief conversation said he was ready to go.

"I'm going to see a retired policeman, at his home, and you can't come in with me," I warned him.

"No problem. I'll scope out the neighborhood." He waited until I'd negotiated the 45th Street off-ramp and was on I-5 before he said anything else.

"Nearly forgot why I was over at your place," he said suddenly. "Janay's mother thinks maybe she saw the killer last night."

"What! Did she tell you that?"

"Nope, told that cop friend of yours. Morgan. But Janay told me. Her mother took her over to her aunt's house this morning; she don't want her alone with a killer around." He shrugged. "She's got the idea there's a fiend wandering the neighborhood. No use telling her it was a premeditated job and the killer was after Mrs. Swallow, nobody else. She's the nervous type."

"What did she tell Sam Morgan?" I demanded. "What did she see? And when?"

"She says ten minutes to twelve. Said she had gone to bed about ten-thirty but she couldn't get to sleep so she finally got up and went into the bathroom to get a sleeping pill. Window in there looks out on Mrs. Swallow's backyard. Said she glanced out and saw somebody on the back porch but thought it was Mrs. Swallow letting her cat in. Forgot all about it until she got home from work last night and Janay told her what had happened."

"If she thought it was Ruth it must have been a woman."

"No, she says not. Said all she was a figure. She thought it was Mrs. Swallow at the time just because it was her house but says it was just a dark blob. No telling whether it was a man or woman because of the trees but after she thought about it some she was sure it was someone bigger than Mrs. Swallow. Looking down, though, and though the trees, it'd be pretty hard to tell how big he was."

Big? there were several large men in the Swallow family, starting with Junior. Nor was Jordan small.

Chapter Sixteen

Leon Kieski lived in a small 1930s-style house on a quiet back street at the east side of Everett. Both the house and yard looked a bit neglected compared to the other houses on the street. There were no signs of children in the neighborhood, no basketball hoops, bicycles, or toy wagons. It was an old neighborhood so possibly most occupants were seniors.

Kieski was somewhat of a surprise. He answered the doorbell so quickly I decided he'd been watching for me out the window. He was very tall, at least six-foot-three, very thin and bony, with high color and a full head of snow-white hair.

"Mr. Kieski, I'm Demary Jones," I said, tilting my head back to look up at him. Five-foot-two has its disadvantages.

"I figured," he said brusquely, stepping back as he motioned me inside. "Come on in. Is that your boy out there?" He nodded at Joey who was lounging against the front fender, watching us.

"No. A friend. He came along for the ride," I said,

wondering at his stiff, almost wary, demeanor. Nobody had forced him to see me. But maybe he was just chary of having a strange woman in his house.

"Well, he's welcome to come in and have a glass of lemonade."

"Thanks, but we stopped at a drive-in on the way up."

He nodded again and shut the door. "Come in then and sit down."

There was no hall so we were already in a small front room that was overfurnished with tired old furniture and a complex TV, VCR, and CD system. The only comfortable-looking chair in the room was a recliner facing the TV, so I sat on the couch. The room was tidy but the couch, and in fact the whole room with the exception of the recliner, was covered with a thick film of dust.

"The woman I talked to said you are looking into the old Swallow case," he said as he sat. Apparently he was a man who didn't waste time on trivialities.

"Well, yes and no." I explained about Birdie and how I'd become involved. "I know, and I've told my friend, that the chances of my discovering anything new about the case are highly unlikely but I did promise her I'd give it a try, so that's what I'm doing."

He smiled faintly. "You don't have to soft-soap me. I don't think we missed anything but it wouldn't matter if we did. Rosellen Swallow was committed so we simply quit working on the case. Easier on the family to simply let it drop. It isn't closed, but unless Mrs. Swallow is released, which is unlikely, there was no point in wasting any more time on it."

"Isn't that unusual?"

He shrugged. "No, not really. The county didn't have a big force and if I remember right we had three other murders we were working on at the time. We concentrated on those." He suddenly gave me a sharp look. "If you came up here thinking I was responsible for dropping the investigation, think again. The case was assigned to me but Captain Clinton made the decisions. Or passed on the chief's."

"Do you know who actually decided not to pursue the inquiry?"

He tilted his head, studying the ceiling. "No," he said finally. "I don't for a positive fact, but I do know Clinton was good buddies with Howard Swallow. Not the victim, his son. They went to school together. But nobody disagreed. There was no point in going on."

"You were that sure she was guilty? What proof did you have?"

He thought again, staring at the ceiling, but not as if he were trying to remember. I was pretty sure he was deciding what to tell me.

"What are you really after?" he asked, bringing his sharp blue gaze down to my face. "Clinton is gone, killed in a small plane crash ten years ago, and the chief has retired. Lives back in Minnesota some place. So if you're thinking to prove malfeasance on their part, or mine, you're wasting your time."

I kept my expression bland but it was a struggle. He might as well have come right out and told me something unethical, if not actually illegal, had been done. Nothing else accounted for his attitude.

"I didn't have anything like that in mind," I said calmly. "I came, as I've already said, because my friend Barbara Swallow asked me to. She doesn't think her grandmother is guilty and she'd like to get her out of the institution she's in."

"What do you think?" he demanded.

I let my surprise show. "I don't think anything. I knew Birdie's grandmother was in an institution but I never heard why until last week. And in case you have the notion I'm some kind of a hotdog private investigator, let me tell you, I'm not. Ninety percent of my work is genealogy. I do have a license but I got it years ago because my boss at that time was a PI and he insisted I get one."

I didn't tell him the only reason I kept my license up was because it bugged Sam. You don't need a license to ask questions.

"Well, I'm sorry for your friend but if she's smart she'll tell you to drop it. Rosellen Swallow was—is— guilty and she's better off in Steilacoom than she'd be in Walla Walla."

I wondered if that was just an offhand remark or if he didn't know she was in a private institution. Whatever, it was obvious I wasn't going to learn anything from Leon Kieski. I wasn't sure why he had agreed to see me; most likely he just wanted to find out what I was doing, or trying to do. He'd certainly never meant to give me any information. He had, however, even if he hadn't intended to.

There had definitely been something underhanded, something questionable, about the way Rosellen had been bundled into Windsor House, and I had every intention, now, of finding out what that was.

Joey was already in the car when Kieski showed me to the door. He was looking straight ahead through the windshield and didn't turn his head until we were well away from the house. He glanced back then, a quick snap of his head.

"Don't wander around," he said sharply. "Make a

straight line back to the freeway and keep going but watch the speed limit. Stay well under."

"What? What are you talking about? What's the matter?"

"I spotted a state trooper parked around the corner from Kieski's house. Unmarked car but he was in uniform and no reason for him to be sitting there. He's hanging a couple of blocks back now. Dark blue Ford. See it?"

I glanced in my rearview mirror. The car was there all right.

I made my sedate way to the closest arterial and headed for I-5. The blue Ford stayed a block behind me. I concentrated on my driving, not thinking about why he was there. I'd do that when I lost him which I did soon after I hit the freeway. Not because of any clever moves on my part, however. He followed for about five miles and then swung off.

Joey breathed a small sigh of relief, surprising me. He wasn't the timid type and I hadn't done anything wrong. There was a strong possibility the Ford hadn't been following us at all. He could have been in the neighborhood for any number of reasons and took the same route I had to the freeway simply because it was the most direct way. On the other hand, we were out of our own territory.

"I didn't get his name," Joey said as the Ford turned into the Mukilteo off-ramp. "But I did get the license."

"He probably didn't have anything to do with—"

"Try that on again," Joey interrupted smugly. "He was in Kieski's house up till about fifteen minutes before we got there, and he is one tough-looking dude, believe me."

I did a mental double-take. I didn't ask him if he was

sure. He would have said so if he wasn't. "Who told you?" I asked instead.

"Lady watering her lawn across the street."

Joey has an uncanny way with older ladies. They like him, trust him, and tell him anything he wants to know.

"Has he been there before?"

"She doesn't remember ever seeing him around any other time. Says he came about forty-five minutes before we did. Parked in front of Kieski's house and went in. Stayed twenty minutes, half hour maybe, then came out again and moved his car around the corner."

He stopped, waited for me to say something, then went on. "Kind of silly. Like some old-time movie. Kieski knew who you were, knew you were coming. Why have somebody follow you out of town?"

I'd have liked the answer to that one myself and wondered if there was any way he could have known that Jake had given me a copy of the Swallow investigation file. He was retired but still seemed to have connections. It wouldn't do Jake any good if Kieski knew what he'd done.

Chapter Seventeen

Martha had arranged another appointment for me that I could catch on my way home. It was for one-thirty with Olin Peterson, who had been a bank officer in Howard's bank at the time of Howard's death. I'd seen his name penciled in the margin of one of Kieski's reports and Martha had traced him. Now, no longer in banking, he was the manager of a small strip-mall in the Bothell district at the north end of Lake Washington.

It was a few minutes after noon when I took the 405 off-ramp and the 527 cutoff to Bothell.

"You hungry?" I asked Joey, who was staring out the window whistling tunelessly. "I'm going to find the mall where the man I want to see works. There should be some places to eat around it. Anything special you'd like?"

"Taco place?"

"Suits me."

I had a bean burrito and a diet cola. Joey washed four tacos down with a double vanilla shake. Teenaged boys have healthy appetites. I left him working on a fifth taco when I walked across the street to the mall.

Peterson was an attractive man somewhere in his early fifties. We met, as agreed, in the office of the mall, where he greeted me pleasantly and after inviting me to sit down asked where I came across his name. Martha had told him it concerned Howard Swallow's death.

"I'm surprised you ever heard of me," he said. "I wasn't sure the police paid any attention to my call. I didn't have anything to do with the investigation but I did contact them after I heard Howard had been killed within a few days of the first of June. I knew that wasn't possible."

I raised my eyebrows. "Not possible? Why not?"

"Because I talked to him on the fifteenth, I think it was. I'm not sure now of the exact date but I knew at the time and it was just two days before the bodies were found."

"You saw him two days before they found his body?" That was a stunner. But now that he'd said so I remembered Birdie telling me that Howard had spoken to his banker on the fifteenth. The reports Jake had given me, however, stated positively that Howard hadn't been seen nor heard from after the first of June. "Where did you see him?" I asked.

"No, no. I didn't see him, I spoke to him. He called the bank; it was a long-distance call. He wanted to talk to Peter Newell. Peter was a senior bank officer, the one Howard always dealt with."

"And Peter talked with him, too?"

"Peter was out to lunch just then so Howard said he'd call back. At the time I presumed he did, particularly so when I didn't hear from the police again. I supposed they had talked to Peter but thinking about it this morning I don't remember his ever saying."

"Is he still with the bank?"

"I certainly doubt it. He was an older man. In his late forties or early fifties then. I was transferred not long after that, to a small town in eastern Washington which, as it turned out, neither I nor my wife liked. I quit banking a year later and although we moved back over here I didn't get back in touch with my former coworkers, so I don't really know about Peter."

"You're sure it was Howard Swallow you talked to?

"Sure? If you mean I could positively identify his voice, no. I hardly knew him. I'd spoken to him a few times in the bank or on the phone but that was all. He sounded familiar, said he was Howard Swallow, and asked to speak with his regular bank officer, so I naturally supposed he was who he said he was."

I thought about that for a moment. I'd have to see if Martha could find Peter Newell. If he had spoken with Howard also on that date, there was definitely something wrong.

"Do you remember the name of the police officer you talked to?" I asked.

He frowned, thinking. "No, I don't. In fact, I'm not sure I ever heard his name. I asked for the officer in charge of the Swallow case, they transferred me, and I— Wait. I do remember, he introduced himself, it was a Captain Clinton. I told him what I've told you."

"And that was the last you heard about it?"

"Yes. As far as I can remember anyway."

"Didn't that surprise you?"

He rolled a pencil between his palms, staring at the wall behind me. "I don't know," he said finally. "I suppose I may have been surprised but my wife and I were expecting our first baby right then and I was more concerned about her than anything else. She was having a rough time. I do recall I was surprised, shocked actually, when they arrested Mrs. Swallow. I did know her, she was often in the bank, and I couldn't believe she'd done it. She was a lovely little lady."

"That seems to have been the opinion of a number of people." Unfortunately not the right people, though, I thought wryly.

I dropped Joey off at his house and got back to the office at two-thirty. Martha was listening on the phone and beavering away on her computer at the same time, several red lights were blinking on the console, the printer was spewing out reams of paper, and the fax machine was chattering like a demented squirrel.

"Good grief, what's going on?" I asked. "Are we under attack or something?"

She nodded at a pile of papers on the end of her desk, her fingers still flying over her keyboard as she transcribed what she was hearing in her headset.

I picked up the papers and started to read. They were the credit reports I asked for on several of the Swallow family members. They reminded me of something Ruth had said when talking about the diary last week. She had commented that all the Wyndlows had an excellent head for finance and that Rosellen, born a Wyndlow, had been no exception. "Those figures in the diary don't necessarily have anything to do with the missing money," she'd said quietly, her eyes on Rosellen who was standing a few feet away just out of earshot. "They could easily be a code for longtime investments."

After looking at the credit reports I thought the present generation of Swallows had certainly missed out on the financial gene. They could have used a little of that expertise. They seemed more interested in spending than earning. They were all in debt, some seriously so. It was no wonder they wanted the house sold.

"I've been getting answers this morning to every query I've sent out in the last month," Martha said when she took off her headset. "I swear, you'd think I was offering backhanders."

"Backhanders?"

"Bribes."

I grinned. "You do."

"Only sometimes," she said, wrinkling her nose at me. "But, believe it or not, I had a bag lady in here this morning thinking the same thing." She laughed. "Honestly, you wouldn't have believed her. Funny shriveled-up little thing in the most awful clothes. Pushing a grocery cart full of junk." She stopped, frowning. "She must have just nicked it. It was one of the new ones from QFC."

"What did she want?"

"Money, of course. She said she heard we paid money for finding out stuff. Her words, not mine, and what did we want to find out."

"You're kidding me. What did you tell her?"

"I gave her five dollars and told her to scarper." She made a moue of distaste. "She had her grubby little hands all over the place. I had to wash everything down after she left."

"Really, Martha, don't you have any sense at all? Five dollars! She'll be back every time you turn around."

"Probably, but she did look pitiful, poor little thing."

Laughing, I was starting into my own office when Anna Carmine came striding down the hall. "Martha, can you possibly type up these papers for me?" she asked, handing her a sheaf of scribbled-on sheets. "I've got an appointment in just twenty minutes and I've got to have these ready for Judge Crowder by five-thirty or I'll have to ask for a postponement. I'll come back and pick them up on my way downtown."

Martha gave them a look and after a quick glance at me, said she would have them ready. "What happened to your new clerk who was supposed to come to work Monday?" she asked.

"Silly little twit broke her leg water-skiing. I have a temp coming in tomorrow." She whipped around and started back down the hall. "Demary, if you're still here when I get back I'll tell you what Professor Bacon had to say about that law firm you wanted information on," she called back over her shoulder. "I talked to him this morning. Kind of interesting." The back door slammed and she was gone.

Chapter Eighteen

Martha handed me a stack of message memos and several pages of fax printouts. "Here's the stuff you need to get that La Rocque history ready to mail, and Captain Nordan called, wanted to know if I'd heard from you. He wasn't best pleased when I told him the trip had been delayed but that I'd have you call as soon as you could. Before you do anything else, though, call Jake." She glanced at her watch. "He'll be home for another forty-five minutes. He doesn't want you to call his office."

"Did he say what about?" I asked, wondering what new information he had for me. Or—an unpleasant thought hit my mind—could he be getting some flak because of my interview with Kieski? So soon? It didn't seem likely.

Likely or not, he had heard from his captain.

"What the heck have you been doing, Demary?" he asked as soon as I said hello. "I thought you said you were just looking into that old homicide for your friend Birdie Swallow. I got the captain climbing all over me, wanting to know why I pulled the Swallow case files."

"Jake, I'm sorry. Are you in serious trouble?"

"Shoot, no. I been doing my job, scanning in the old files, nothing else. Just happened to take the Swallow files next." He laughed. "At least that's all anybody can prove. But what stirred him up? What kind of a hornet's nest were you poking around in?"

"I'll be darned if I know. I talked to Leon Kieski this morning; he was the investigating officer, but that shouldn't have bothered anybody. Besides, he's retired. And he sure couldn't have known I got any information from you. Actually, we didn't even discuss the case. He more or less told me to mind my own business and that was that." I stopped and thought a second. "Do you suppose it was because of Ruth Swallow's murder? The captain's interest in the Swallow files, I mean. Her ex-husband is an attorney there in Everett."

"Ruth Swallow? When did she get it? He didn't mention her. I don't know anything about that one."

"She was killed Monday night, here in Seattle. Somebody stabbed her to death right in her own bed. Less than a mile from here, in fact."

"Monday night! I thought you meant another one twenty years ago. That must be what it was about. Nothing to do with you at all. Who has the Swallow investigation?"

"Sam."

"Oh, boy. Demary, you better back off the whole thing before you give poor Sam a coronary."

"Fat chance! I'm looking at Birdie's grandfather's death, and that case is over twenty years old, so why should I back off? But I did learn one thing from Kieski. Not that he actually told me anything but I could tell from his attitude that there was something illegal, immoral, or off-color somehow with the way Rosellen

Swallow was bundled into Windsor House. And I'm going to find out what it was whether anybody likes it or not."

He laughed. "At any rate it sounds as if you—"

"Wait a minute," I interrupted him. "I just remembered something. The guy who followed us. Kieski must have set that up."

"What guy? When?"

"He followed us from Kieski's house." I told him about the blue Ford and gave him the license number.

"H-m-m. The captain didn't mention Kieski, so I doubt if it was anything to do with the department, but why would Kieski have somebody follow you at all? Strange. I'll check the plate though. It might tell us something."

"Don't get yourself in a bind over this, Jake. You're new up there; you don't know whose toes you might be stepping on."

He laughed again. "If I step hard enough maybe we'll learn why the guy was following you," he said as he rang off.

Jake never lets little things like his boss's displeasure bother him.

I started to call Captain Nordan next to let him know why I hadn't gotten to Alaska as planned but the phone rang again immediately.

"I nearly forgot," Jake said quickly when I picked up. "I got two more names for you. They were interviewed by a different detective working the case and were in another folder I pulled last night. One is Berthe Anderson; she was a part-time housekeeper for the Swallows at the time of the murder, and the other is Cyndie Dancer. Probably a stage name. She was Dian Clark's roommate. They both worked for a small circus or carnival called Wellington's Wonder Show. There isn't any other information on her or the circus but Anderson still lives here in Everett. She's in the book. Neither one of them had anything pertinent to say when they were questioned back then, but you might get something out of them now. I gotta go." He hung up with a crash.

"What was that all about?" Martha asked, coming in with another bunch of faxes for me to look at.

I asked her to sit for a minute and gave her a quick rundown on my conversations with Leon Kieski and Olin Peterson, and both conversations with Jake.

She rubbed her forehead with her fingertips. "The more you learn, or hear about, the way Rosellen was placed in Windsor, the more rogue it sounds. What I can't understand is why everyone went along. Birdie wasn't old enough to do any protesting but her mother certainly was. I only met her one time when she was in here with Birdie but she didn't strike me as a woman who would agree to putting her mother in a loony bin unless she had to. There was the sister too. Alison. Junior couldn't have engineered it on his own." She stopped, frowning. "Do you suppose she actually was guilty?"

"Nothing I've learned says so. If she was, there was certainly nothing in the file, nor anywhere else that I know of that pointed to her particularly. The only physical evidence they had against her was her fingerprints on the pipe and those were easily explained. The DA would never have taken the case to court on that alone. He couldn't have gotten a conviction. Besides, there were a half dozen other prints on the thing."

Martha mumbled something.

"What? I didn't get that."

"I said this isn't getting us anywhere, we've already been over it before." She stood up. "I'll see if I can locate those two women for you. Maybe one of them knows something they didn't tell the coppers at the time."

She straightened the Japanese wall hanging as she went out. The poor thing was getting lopsided from her straightening.

I booted up my desktop and brought the Swallow case on screen. The credit reports on the various members of the family reminded me of the one thing I hadn't considered. Who, if anyone, benefited in a material way from Howard's death? In my opinion most murders were committed for one of three reasons. Fear, gain of some kind, or accident, with gain being number one. After this long a time it might be hard to uncover who feared or hated Howard enough to kill him, the reason, or reasons, were too far in the past, but it shouldn't be too difficult to find out who had benefited. Money left a paper trail that was hard to conceal. As many a tax evader had found out to his or her sorrow.

I worked on the money angle for the next hour, accessing a few data bases but mostly working off the credit reports and making lists of what I needed to look for and where to do my looking. Anna stuck her head in the door a few minutes before five and said she'd be back in a half hour if I wanted to wait for her. I said I'd be waiting.

Martha went home, reminding me again before she left to call Captain Nordan.

He picked up on the second ring. I explained what had happened and told him I would fly up, probably next week. He didn't like that and was rude about it, surprising me. I'd never actually met him but as far as I could tell from my two other conversations with him there was nothing pressing about the research. He wasn't that far along with his story outline. His attitude irritated me but he'd sent me a good-sized retainer check so I smoothed his feathers and we hung up on a reasonably pleasant note.

Thinking about him later, however, I had an unpleasant thought. From the beginning he'd been very specific about what he wanted me to do, starting with locating the man I was to see in Ketchikan. He had twice asked me if I had an exact address on him.

Once before, when I'd first been on my own, I'd been hired by someone who had eventually been arrested for stalking the woman I'd located for him. From then on I've been very careful about that kind of a job but I'd never thought of it in connection with Captain Nordan because the person he wanted found was a man. The idea seemed a little far-fetched but I'd get Martha do a background check on Nordan before I went to Alaska.

I put the thought aside and returned to the Swallows' finances until Anna came back at six-fifteen.

She flopped into one of the tangerine-colored chairs and kicked off her shoes. "This has been an absolute horror of a day," she said with a sigh of relief. "I've been on the dead run since seven o'clock this morning. My feet are killing me, I haven't had anything to eat since the bagel I ate at dawn, and Judge Crowder is a pain in the you-know-what."

I grinned. "I take it you missed his five-thirty deadline."

"I didn't, he did. He was gone and the old buzzard left word with his clerk that I was postponed for ten days. I didn't want a postponement, darn it. I've been clearing my desk to go on vacation. Now I've got to rearrange my whole schedule. Oh, well, you don't want to listen to me moan. Let's go have dinner and I'll tell you what Professor Bacon had to say about Howard Swallow. Almost none of which was very complimentary."

Chapter Nineteen

We went to the Salmon House, one of my favorites, and got a window table where I could look out at the streamlined shape of the old *Kalakala*. It was tied up across the way at the Professional Marine Company's moorage while it was slowly being restored to its former glory. Even in her rust-streaked condition the big ferry was beautiful.

It made me think of Captain Nordan again and I reminded myself to make sure of a background check on him.

Our waitress's name was Carolyn. I'd met her, briefly, some time ago working on another case. She had an old-time hourglass figure and sensational legs. Every unattached male in the place eyed her progress around the room.

When she had taken our order and moved off Anna slumped back in her chair and took a sip of the "restorative" martini she'd ordered. "Well, what do you want to know first?" she asked.

"Anything at all. Start at the top. How did he react to

your first question about the firm? Or Howard. Did he remember the case?"

"I don't think the old boy has forgotten anything, including the weather reports, since he was six," she said with obvious admiration. "Unfortunately, as far as the case itself is concerned he doesn't know anything other than what was in the papers. He wasn't involved and the Seattle papers had other priorities. The firm, Wellman, Bowers and Cranmer, was a different story. He knew all the partners in a personal, if distant way."

"Great."

"For your purposes I'm not too sure of that. Not if you're looking for something too negative anyway. I was wrong about one of them being a student of his though. He had Cranmer's son in one of his classes. He also knew Howard, the present Howard, the one you called Junior. He attended several of Bacon's seminars. As he said, he couldn't speak for Junior's probity, only his competence, which he said was above the norm. But that was as a student, not as a practicing attorney. The firm as a whole, on the other hand, he considered well above the average and above reproach."

I frowned. "I thought you said earlier that he wasn't entirely complimentary about them."

"He wasn't. The above was strictly de jure. Competent according to the law. That type of competence has never been high on Bacon's list. As he says, anyone can learn to look up the pertinent law for whatever tort, civil suit, or whatever, that he's working on. The trick is in learning how to present the facts, or lack thereof, to judge or jury in order to win your case. In other words, he considered both the firm and Junior plodding. Following the letter rather than the intent of the law and with no flair."

"That's interesting."

Anna raised her eyebrows in query. "How so?"

I grinned. "Because that was my opinion of Junior right off. Maybe that was why he didn't go in for criminal law as Birdie said he started out to do."

"Possibly, but I think maybe the switch to civil was because of one of his cases Bacon told me about. Mainly to illustrate his point regarding plodding. Junior took a case involving a distant relative named Jordan Wyndlow. You know who he is?"

"Yes, I've met him."

"Well, sometime after the murder, six months or so, Wyndlow went on trial for assault with intent to kill, and Junior lost the case. Spectacularly. It never even went to the jury."

I stared at her wide-eyed. "But . . . but Sam told me he'd never served time."

"He didn't. Believe it or not the judge threw the case out. Bacon said Junior did such a lousy job Wyndlow would have been acquitted on appeal anyway. The judge would have been in line for a reprimand if he'd let the trial proceed. Plus the reputation of the woman involved made her testimony a joke to start with. She had previously accused at least four other men of much the same thing. All of whom proved her a liar. That did not come out at the trial, of course, but the judge did know it."

"Well, that sure answers one thing for me."

"What?" Anna leaned back to let Carolyn deposit her salad in front of her.

I told her about Jordan's cottage. "Junior either has a guilty conscience or Jordan may have some kind of proof that Junior blew the case deliberately."

"Could be. Bacon was surprised that there were no further developments."

"Junior's lack of skill may be why Rosellen is in

Windsor," I said thoughtfully, taking a bite of the marinated asparagus salad I'd ordered.

She shook her head. "No, there was something else going on. I don't know what but it's highly unlikely that she would have been committed simply because he didn't know what he was doing. No judge would sign a commitment order without expert psychiatric evaluation if there was any sign of incompetence, or malfeasance, on the part of the attorney, and you say there is no record of a psychiatrist being involved at all."

"Not as far as I can tell from any of the records I've gotten a hold of yet. But I'm thinking now that they are incomplete. There must be more somewhere. Competency hearings aren't sealed, are they?"

She shrugged. "Some are, some aren't. Depends on the judge, the jurisdiction, what's involved, age of the defendant, any number of things. Doesn't Birdie or her mother know?"

"Birdie doesn't and everyone else just tells me to back off."

"They must not know you very well," she said with a grin. "Telling you to back off almost guarantees you'll keep going."

An hour later we had finished our dinner—cold dilled salmon, pan-fried new potatoes drizzled with olive oil, and a baby-vegetable medley—and were lingering over a last cup of Starbucks coffee when I got a gut-wrenching surprise. I looked over toward the entryway just in time to see Sam standing there with a beautiful brunette woman, and to see him brush her cheek with a light kiss as he waited for the maître d' to show them to a table.

I was so shocked I didn't even have the presence of

mind to turn my head but fortunately they were shown to the dining area on the other side of the entryway.

"What's the matter, Demary?" Anna asked in alarm, seeing my expression.

I managed some kind of explanation without mentioning Sam and within a few minutes we were on our way out. We had come in Anna's car so she took me back to the office where I'd left my old Toyota. I know we talked on the way but I didn't remember a word of it and switched cars in a sort of dumb fog.

I was home in the kitchen, and for some unknown reason drinking a glass of buttermilk, before I came out of it enough to get mad.

At myself.

What in the world was the matter with me? Sam didn't owe me anything. Nor I him, as I'd told him any number of times. I'd certainly had enough dates with other men—what made me think I had the right to expect anything different from Sam? We weren't engaged, or anything else. He had a perfect right to take a beautiful brunette to dinner. And to kiss her cheek in public.

He'd never kissed my cheek in public.

With that thought I burst into tears.

Chapter Twenty

I woke the next morning, after very little sleep, still mad at myself, Sam, and the world in general. A really stupid frame of mind. But at least I did recognize it and by the time I showered, dressed—in a bronze-colored cotton pants suit with a pale yellow top—and had a cup of coffee, I was doing better.

At some point during the night, to get my mind off Sam and the brunette, I'd turned the light on and written myself a list of what I wanted to do today. I keep a notepad and pencil on my bedside table for jotting down my middle-of-the-night ideas. Some of them are pretty good. One of the first things on my agenda this morning was getting a title search done on the Swallow property. I had assumed it was still in Rosellen's name, or hers and Howard's, but that wasn't necessarily true and it might be interesting to see just what the status of the place was, and what the assessed value was also.

I got to the office about a minute before Martha did. She came in with an armful of printed material that she immediately handed to me.

"Some professor friend of Charles gave him all this stuff. A Dick Larsen, Larkin, something like that. Charles must have told him you were interested in the *Kalakala*. He didn't remember doing so, but you know Charles."

I did indeed know Charles. He is the quintessential absentminded professor. He is well known as one of the best in his field, medieval English literature, but once off that subject he is so vague he drives me crazy. Martha is so sharp, so quick, I've often wondered what attracted them to each other.

The bulk of material in the pile surprised me. In addition to a stack of Internet printouts and newspaper clippings, there were several notebook-sized publications at least an inch thick that contained pictures, diagrams of the decks, specifications on various kinds of machinery, and lengthy histories. There was also a small hardcover book called *The Silver Beauty*, a gossipy year-by-year history of the *Kalakala*, starting with the laying of her keel in 1925.

There was so much information I wondered again about Captain Nordan. What kind of a book was he supposedly writing? It didn't look as if the *Kalakala* needed another history.

"Martha, come in here a minute," I called. I told her my problem with Nordan and asked her to start a background on him before she did anything else. "I'm beginning to wonder if I haven't already made a serious mistake in telling him about Gunner." Johan Gunner was the man I'd located in Ketchikan whose father had worked on the *Kalakala*.

"Did you tell him Gunner's name?" she asked.

"No. I wasn't sure about him yet. Gunner, I mean."

"Good thing, maybe," Martha said thoughtfully. She

started out and then turned back. "I nearly forgot. I called Berthe Anderson before I went home yesterday and left a message on her answering machine. She left an answer on ours sometime last night. She will be home by one-thirty this afternoon and will see you then. Do you want me to say okay?"

I had to grin. "Yep, tell the machine I'll be there. Where does she live?"

"I thought Jake said she still lived in Everett but the address she gave me is in Montlake Terrace. Do you want me to print you out a street map?"

"H-m-m, yes. Might be a good idea. I don't know the area."

After she'd left I called a real estate broker I knew, Penny Sawyer, and asked her to do a title search on the Swallow property for me, including the piece with Jordan's house. I knew she could do it better than I could and she owed me a favor. A couple of years ago I'd stumbled on some information that had kept her from joining a commercial venture that would have bankrupted her and warned her off in time to let her bow out gracefully. It had been a small thing from my point of view—I'd come across the information by accident—but she was forever grateful.

"I'm sorry I don't have the parcel number on the place, just the address," I told her.

"No problem, just takes a bit longer," she said. "Is this something to do with the murder?"

"Whose murder?" I asked, swallowing a gasp of surprise. How in the world did she know about Howard and Dian's death. She wasn't old enough.

"Ruth Swallow's murder," she replied, sounding puzzled. "She was killed just a couple of blocks from you. It's been in all the papers."

"Oh, of course, I wasn't thinking." I'd temporarily forgotten Ruth. "No, it has nothing to do with her but she was married to one of the family. Used to be, I mean. And there is a murder involved, two in fact, but they took place twenty-two years ago. That's what I'm working on, and at the moment I'm just fishing."

"Three murders? In one family? Isn't that a bit unusual? Not a family I'd care to be a part of. Too hazardous."

Put like that, it was a bit unusual. Plus the fact that both killings—I was lumping Howard and Dian together—were skewed somehow. Ruth's death sent a frisson of horror down my back every time I thought of it.

I sat and thought about that for a while after we hung up, wondering if Sam had checked all the family alibis yet. I reached for the phone to call him and then jerked my hand away as if I'd been stung.

I'd forgotten the brunette. For a moment I was close to tears again, which infuriated me. What *was* the matter with me?!

Berthe Anderson's address was a tiny cottagelike house tucked behind a screen of huge laurels. The place reminded me a bit of Jordan's house, flower-covered and immaculate. A picture-postcard kind of place. Berthe, however, did not match the house. In fact, when she opened the door I thought at first that she must be a friend or neighbor. For one thing she was a big, folksy-looking woman, five-nine or -ten, and weighed at least two-fifty, too large for her surroundings. Her hair, a graying blond, was pulled back off her face into a bun that had deteriorated into a scraggly bundle of floating wisps, some of which were sticking to her sweaty neck. She was wearing a pair of none-too-clean violet stretch pants and a green T-shirt that had seen better days. Her feet were bare, shoved into a pair of rubber thongs that were too small for her.

"C'mon in," she said, backing up to give me room after I'd introduced myself. "I just got in myself. I'm having a Coors before I take a shower. I'm beat. Want a beer? Or how about having lunch with me? I bought a fresh crab on the way home."

"Crab sounds really good. I'd love it," I said. "But go ahead and drink your beer. My questions can wait."

She ushered me through the hall and into the front room. A small but beautiful room with a chintz-covered couch and chairs, a polished coffee table with a bowl of fresh flowers on it, two side tables, also with flowers, and a graceful curio cabinet full of what looked like antique Minton willow ware.

"Beautiful place," I said, glancing around.

"Bit frilly for my taste. It's my sister's house. She and her husband are off on vacation so I'm house-sitting. I'm working on a pigsty of a job just a couple blocks away over in Briar so it's convenient too. Couple of kids, renters, trashed the place before they left."

"How about your husband? You left him home?"

"I don't have one," she said motioning me toward one of the chairs. "I never found a guy I thought was worth the effort of training."

I raised my eyebrows, smiling. "Never?"

She laughed goodnaturedly. "There were a few possibles. I tried them on for size, so to speak, but ended up throwing them back."

"Girl after my own heart," I said, laughing too.

"Your message said you wanted to see me about the Swallows. I haven't worked for them for twenty years," Berthe said, finishing off the rest of her can of beer as she started toward the hall. "I'm not sure I remember much about them. I was just a kid at the time. Eighteen or nineteen." She laughed harshly. "I do remember Rosellen, though. She's the one who did the killings."

I swallowed. Berthe didn't sound as if she were repeating rumor or gossip—she sounded as if she'd seen what happened, knew for a fact that Rosellen was guilty.

Chapter Twenty-one

Berthe looked a different person when she came back downstairs dressed in white shorts and a pink-striped shirt, and with her clean-washed hair in a ponytail.

"Man, do I ever feel better," she said as she sat down at the kitchen table. "Those kids left that house in the worst mess I ever saw. I don't think they even bothered to pick up anything they dropped on the floor. If the dog didn't eat it they kicked it into a corner. Disgusting! I wouldn't be doing the job for anyone but Mae. Hand me another can of beer out of the refrigerator and let's eat. I'm starved."

I was hungry too and lost no time following her example. At her suggestion I had put plates, silverware, lettuce, crab, mayonnaise, horseradish, and a loaf of French bread out on the kitchen table while she was showering.

"Who's Mae?" I asked around a mouthful of crab piled with mayo and horseradish. "An elderly aunt?"

"Yes, she is. How did you guess? Well, actually, she's my mother's cousin but I call her my aunt. She has several small rentals that supply most of her income. I take care of them for her. These two brats that rented the place are shirt-tail relatives, too, and when I get my hands on them they're going to be sorry they ever set foot in the place, to say nothing of what they did to it."

We applied ourselves to the crab for the next few minutes. Fresh Dungeness crab is true ambrosia, God's gift from the sea.

"Well, what's your interest in the Swallows?" Berthe asked when we finally sat back from the feast. "What are you? A real estate broker, or what?"

"I'm sorry," I said, surprised. "I thought Martha told you. I'm a friend of Barbara Swallow. Do you remember her?"

She looked blank for a moment and then nodded. "Yes, I do. Cute little blond kid. They called her Birdie then."

"She still is and they still do," I said, smiling, and went on to tell her how I got involved.

We rinsed the dishes and put them in the dishwasher as I talked. When the kitchen was tidy we went back to the front room, Berthe with a fresh can of beer and me with a glass of cold lemonade.

"You sound very sure of Rosellen's guilt," I said as I sat down in the corner of the couch. I didn't see any coasters so I hung on to my glass, not wanting to leave any circles on that shining coffee table. "What makes you think that way?"

She shrugged. "The way she acted, I suppose. The way the whole family acted. I only worked one day a week but it happened to be the day the neighbor man, I think his name was Johnson, found their bodies." She stopped, turning her beer can round and round between her hands. "I remember that day ver-r-y clearly. As I said, I wasn't much more than a kid, so when the police came it was exciting rather than anything else as far as I was concerned. I hadn't seen Mr. Swallow more than a dozen times in the six months I'd worked there so he didn't mean much to me."

"Did the police question you?"

"Sure." She grinned. "I was so thrilled it's a wonder I was even coherent. I probably wasn't, to start with anyway, but by the time I'd been questioned a dozen times I remember being thoroughly tired of it. I know I decided I didn't want to be a cop anyway. Too boring."

I wondered if she thought cleaning other people's houses a lot of fun. She answered that with her next remark.

"Plus I don't like being told what to do. The head cop ordered the other guys around like he was head of the Gestapo. Cleaning, I'm my own boss and I make more than I could make any other way with my lack of education. School was another thing I didn't like. But to get back to Rosellen Swallow. When Johnson came back, before the police got there, and told her what he'd found, Rosellen ran out to the shed to look in the freezer. She came back screaming like a banshee."

"Didn't Johnson try to stop her?"

"Sure, but she jerked away from him. The thing that has stuck in my mind is that when she came back she wasn't crying, not acting like I expected someone to act after seeing their husband frozen to death in a freezer, just screaming."

"Shock takes different people different ways."

"True. But even now, thinking back, I swear she wasn't grief-stricken, not even really upset."

"I know you said you had hardly even seen Howard

but when you did how did they seem together? Did they seem happy? Or were they having problems?"

She thought about that, frowning. "I'm not sure I'd have known one way or another back then. I certainly don't remember anything out of the ordinary. Except for the gun."

"What gun?" I asked quickly. This was the first mention of a gun I'd heard.

"Little pearl-handled thing. Looked like one of those gambler's hide-out guns you see in cowboy movies. I'd seen it before. Mrs. Swallow kept it in her bedside table. Or on it. The day he, Mr. Swallow, took it away she'd left it on top of her dresser and he came into the bedroom just as I picked it up to put it away. He snatched it away from me and went stomping downstairs. They had an argument about it. I could hear their voices but they weren't yelling so it didn't amount to much. I never saw the gun again, though."

"Do you remember what they said?"

She shook her head. "Too long ago. And as I said it didn't amount to much. A few sharp words from him was about all it was."

"You were doing the bedroom so it must have been late for him to be home at all. Do you remember why he was still there? Or when it was in relation to the time they found the bodies?"

"Yes, I do know that. It was the Tuesday after the Memorial Day weekend and he was packing to go somewhere."

Now that was interesting. It substantiated Rosellen's claim that Howard had gone to San Francisco. "Did you tell the police about him packing, and about the gun? And was it ever found?"

She finished her beer and got up to put the can away.

"It's so long ago I can't really remember what I told them. The packing bit, I don't know, maybe, but it seems like I must have said something about the gun. I don't believe I'd ever even seen a gun before. Since then I've seen stranger things than guns in people's homes but back then it was a real novelty. I don't think I ever heard any more about it though so I don't know if they found it or not."

I followed her into the kitchen and rinsed my lemonade glass while she took the bundled crab shells out to the trash can. The backyard was beautiful, filled with flowering shrubs and beds of brilliantly colored perennials. There was a tiny gazebo in the far corner half covered with a wisteria in full bloom. When I see a yard like that one I'm always tempted to go home and do something exciting with mine. Fortunately the impulse doesn't last. I long ago came to the conclusion that gardening was not for me.

"You know, I've been thinking," Berthe said as she came back inside. "One of the reasons I guess I thought Rosellen Swallow was guilty was the way the three kids acted. Junior and the two girls. I didn't see them until the next week when I came to do the house, which, incidently, was the last time I cleaned for them. I never went back after that day."

"Why not? Did they tell you not?"

"No. Frankly, I didn't like them. The kids. We were all about the same age and to my mind they treated me like a servant, which, again to my mind, I sure as heck wasn't. I thought I was doing them a favor more than anything else so I told them I wouldn't be coming again.

"But anyway, I don't know how they acted when they first heard about their father's death but when I came that one next time the only thing they were interested in was what I'd told the police. All three of them, at different times, caught me alone and that was the first thing they asked. What had I told the police?"

"How did you answer?"

She shrugged. "I don't remember. I just remember being surprised that it was all they wanted to know. They knew I'd been there the week before when the bodies were found but they didn't ask about that at all. They were only interested in what I'd told the cops. Seemed strange to me. Still does."

It seemed strange to me, too.

Chapter Twenty-two

When I left Berthe I went over to a little strip-mall a couple of blocks away and called Jake from a pay phone. I wanted to know if he had read anything about a gun in any of the Swallow reports. He was at work and I didn't want to use my cell phone.

"Never saw a thing about a gun," he told me cheerfully after assuring me no one else was in the office. "None on the properties list, I know that."

"What the heck could have happened to it?" I wondered. "People don't just throw a gun in the trash."

"Think the woman, Berthe, is reliable?"

"Yes. I don't think she was lying anyway. Why should she? No point in it. Doesn't seem like something she would make up either. But I don't know about her memory. For one thing it was twenty-two years ago, and as she said, she was just a kid. At the time she thought finding the bodies was exciting. She couldn't wait to tell her friends all about it but after this long a time she doesn't have any real recollection of what she said to anyone so she doesn't know whether she told the law about the gun or not. She's still clear enough on what she saw, though."

"There might be something in those other reports I told you about yesterday. I ran copies and took them home but I didn't bother looking at them much. Just picked out those two names. I'll be off in an hour though and I've got a big steak in the refrigerator. C'mon up and help me eat it. We can take a look at the files before you take them home with you."

I hesitated. I needed to check in with Martha but decided not to bother. I'd go get the new stuff he'd copied and call it a day. I didn't want anything to eat; I was too full of crab.

On the other hand maybe I'd be hungry again by the time we got around to the steak.

As it turned out I did eat steak, along with a baked potato and a green salad, while we read the reports he'd copied and talked about the case. It was after twelve before I left for home. I wasn't at all tired and when I saw the Edmonds off-ramp coming up I decided to cut over and take a look at the Swallow place.

Everything was dark and quiet when I parked in the drive and shut off my lights. There was no sign of anyone being around. The scene was impossibly beautiful with the moon laying its shimmering white light over the house and grounds. I sat in the car for a while, just looking, then decided to go down to the beach. I didn't bother locking the car, or taking my bag with me. I just got out and wandered past the shed where the freezer had been kept, and on down the path through the shrubbery.

It was a beautiful night, warm and still, with a million stars studding a velvet-black sky. I got as far as the railroad and was standing on the tracks gazing out at the water when something hit the back of my knees a terrifying wallop. I had a second's wonder how any one, or any thing, could have got that close without my sensing them, then I started to fall. Someone hit my shoulders another shattering blow and I went head over heels down the embankment and into the water. The cove is shaped like a sharp pointed V and at the point, where I was, there wasn't any beach at high tide. There was a solid breakwater of huge boulders along the base of the right-of-way, however, and how I managed to sail out and over them I don't know. I hit the water hard, sending it twenty feet into the air around me. It was freezing cold but not very deep and as I scrambled for the surface my feet brushed the sand below me.

I didn't have time to worry about whoever had hit me. I'm a poor swimmer and the undertow was already sucking me out into deep water. I knew if I didn't get back on dry land and do it fast I'd drown. I didn't have the strength to battle the tide.

I didn't know how long I struggled toward the shore; it seemed like hours but it couldn't have been ten minutes at most. I didn't have to swim more than a few feet before I was able to stand and although the undertow kept washing my footing out from underneath me, sending me back under to swallow more saltwater, the oncoming waves shoved me forward just enough that I was able to flounder ashore a hundred yards on down the beach from where I'd gone in. Gasping for air, I crawled a few feet clear of the water before I flopped, exhausted and hurting all over. I didn't know how much time passed but it wasn't long before I had the thought that I'd better convalesce somewhere else. I was all too visible lying spread out there on the sand. Shivering with cold, and shock, I crawled on into the shadow of the rocks and forced myself into a sitting position.

The shivering turned to coughing which brought up some of the seawater I'd swallowed and then I must have passed out. When I opened my eyes again the sky was beginning to get light and a man in swimming trunks was walking across the sand toward me.

My heart slammed against my ribs. For a second I was too terrified to move, then I scrambled to my feet, distantly surprised that I was able to move at all. My whole body hurt and I was shaking with cold.

"Miss Jones? Miss Jones, what are you doing here? And you're wet. What happened to you?" Jordan Wyndlow asked coming to a stop a few feet in front of me. His expression was shocked and concerned.

"I-I . . . some-someone threw me into the water," I stammered, still frightened. Jordan could easily have been the one who did the throwing. "W-what are you doing here?"

"I swim every morning about this time," he said, brushing my question aside. "What do you mean, someone threw you into the water? What were you doing here? I don't understand." He paused, looking at me intently. "Well, that hardly matters at the moment. You need to get warm and dry. Come." He held out his hand. "I'll take you to my place and you can have a hot shower while I find you something dry to wear. You can explain what happened later." He stopped again, frowning slightly. "Do you want me to call the police?"

"N-no. I don't know. . . . No, I-I . . . j-just need to get warm." My teeth were chattering so hard I nearly bit my tongue getting the words out. I didn't have any reason to trust Jordan, nor any reason not to trust him. At the moment all I could think about was getting warm and dry.

I took his hand.

It was broad daylight with a bright sunny day in progress when I sat down at the kitchen table in Jordan's kitchen and took my first sip of the hot sweet tea he'd insisted I drink. In the meantime I'd had a hot, very hot and very long, shower, downed four aspirin, and dressed in an old but clean sweatsuit he said had belonged to a friend. While I was thus occupied Jordan walked over to the big house to retrieve my car. It was parked now in front of the cottage.

"I don't think you had better eat anything like bacon and eggs," he said, handing me a plate with two slices of buttered toast alongside a small bowl of sliced fresh peaches.

I nodded. I didn't really want anything but the tea. I was feeling much better, not anywhere near as sore, but my stomach was still queasy from all the saltwater I'd swallowed.

"Can you tell me now what happened to you?" he asked.

I told him all, finishing with the fact that despite the force of the blow my shoulders didn't look any different than they ever did. I'd looked in the mirror when I dressed.

"You didn't hear anyone?" he asked. "Not before, or after you got out of the water?"

"No, and I don't really understand that. The embankment and between the ties is all gravel. I should have heard him, her, whatever, coming."

"Did you look at your clothes when you took them off?"

"No. I'm sorry," I said. "I just dropped them on the floor and when I went back to—"

"Yes, I went in and picked them up. I wanted to look at them. Your jacket has a long horizontal rip across the shoulders. I think you had an encounter with a black bear, and probably a female with a cub in tow, otherwise she wouldn't have attacked you."

"A bear?" My voice rose.

"Very likely. The cub may have bumped into you first, let out a startled sound of some kind and she charged. There have been several of them around here this spring. I thought they had all been trapped and taken into the mountains but apparently not because I'm pretty sure that's what happened to you. Despite nearly drowning you were actually lucky she didn't do more than take a swipe at you."

Chapter Twenty-three

Jordan had already called some wildlife department and he insisted that I stay and repeat my story to the young man who eventually came to talk to me. I refused to take him back to where it happened because it had been almost exactly at the point of the cove and he could find that for himself. Although I was feeling much better I still felt too sore and lame to want to walk that far.

At first I was furious at him; he was more concerned about possible damage to the bear than he was about damage to me. He was so earnest about it, however, asking if I'd kicked or thrown anything at the animal, that I was finally amused.

"In the first place it happened too fast for me to have done anything, and second, I thought my assailant was human," I told him. I didn't tell him I was still far from convinced that it hadn't been a human. The smash across my back had felt more like a two-by-four than it had like a bear's paw. "I was more concerned with getting away and staying alive than I was in retaliating," I added.

He nodded soberly. "Yes, very frightening being knocked into the water like that."

I agreed wholeheartedly.

I had called Martha while I was waiting for the wild-life man to tell her I'd be late getting in and to tell her why so she was waiting, her smooth chocolate-colored face filled with concern, when I got to the office at eleven-thirty.

And to my concern, Sam was also there.

"What are *you* doing here?" I demanded, sounding like a shrew. And a shrewish wife at that.

"I called; Martha told me what happened," he said, ignoring my tone. "I want to know what you were doing up there at that time of night, and exactly what happened."

"What do you care," I snapped. "And it's none of your business what I was doing up there."

Martha's eyes popped. She started to say something, thought better of it, grabbed some papers off her desk and wheeled away down the hall toward Anna's office.

Sam's voice hardened. "It's very much my business, you silly woman," he said. "I'm investigating a murder connected to that house. I want to know what the heck you were doing prowling around the place. You could have gotten yourself killed."

"Silly? Silly woman?" I yelled, picking up on the only words that registered. "What do you mean, silly woman? What gives you the right to call me anything? Anything at all. I'm not your woman, silly or not!"

That remark stopped both of us dead in our tracks.

Sam turned and walked out, being careful not to touch me as he went past.

"You've either lost your mind or you've found out

Sam is dating someone else," Martha said judiciously from the shelter of the hall. "And if you yell at me I'm going home until you're in a more reasonable frame of mind."

I stood there staring at her. "I just made a darn fool of myself, didn't I?"

"Well, I don't think the Queen is going to present you with an OBE for good sense," she said. "Want to tell me about it? Getting dunked in the Sound that way must have been horrible. You're lucky to still be here, but what else is going on?"

"C'mon in," I said, trudging toward my office. The borrowed sweatsuit had belonged to a much taller woman. The legs dragged on the ground around the borrowed slippers. I looked like a war-zone refugee, which hadn't helped my self-esteem any at seeing Sam.

Martha was not sympathetic. "What's your problem?" she asked after I'd told her about the incident at the Salmon House. "If I heard right you just spent the evening with Jake Allenby. Why are you so bent out of shape over Sam taking this brunette out to dinner?"

"I don't know," I said. "I really don't know. It just upset the heck out of me."

"You need to get back to work and quit brooding," she said astringently. "I located Dian's roommate, Cyndie Dancer. She's here in Seattle, temporarily, and said you could come see her this afternoon. Go home and change your clothes and get on out there. She has a place in the south end, on Pearl Street just off Rainier Avenue."

Cyndie Dancer lived in an apartment on the third floor of a tired-looking building that had been thrown up sometime in the fifties. Painted an ugly shade of brown, and surrounded by half dead shrubs in weed-choked beds, it looked a depressing place to live. There was no security system, anyone could walk in, and from the looks of the narrow foyer it was frequently used as a meeting place by untidy people. The worn tile floor was littered with old takeout sacks, dead leaves, and crumpled balls of unsolicited mail. It smelled of fried cabbage and trash.

No elevator, so I had to trudge up the three flights to Cyndie's door. Despite four more aspirin, another hot shower and a change of clothes I was still sore all over and felt lousy.

I wasn't expecting much so Cyndie was a pleasant surprise when she opened the door in answer to my knock. Small, not much taller than I am, with a trim figure, and a fresh, make-up-free complexion, she was neatly dressed in a jeans and a navy blue T-shirt. I knew she was older than I was but she looked much younger. Actually, she looked like she might be an aerobics instructor; she didn't look like my idea of an ex-circus performer. And after introductions and an invitation to share the pot of coffee she had just made, I told her so.

"Maybe not," she said, smiling. "But that's what I am. Sit down, while I go get us that coffee. I'll be right back."

I chose the chair to one side of the couch and looked around. The room was neat, clean, furnished with obviously secondhand furniture—nothing matched—and totally bare of anything personal. So bare, in fact, it looked like a stage setting. I didn't have time to do more than take in that much before she came back with a thermos pot and two mugs on a tin tray.

"I hope black is okay. I don't have any cream or sugar," she said, setting the tray down on an old army foot-locker that served as a coffee table. "I only moved in here three days ago and I've been too busy to even buy the basics."

"Black is fine," I said, accepting the cup she handed me. "Did Martha tell you why I wanted to see you?"

"Yes. Made me curious. I've wondered for years about her death. That's why I said I'd see you, because to tell the truth I don't really have the time. I've always kept a place in Seattle to come back to but my old apartment building was condemned to make room for another free-way ramp so I had to move. I have to get myself settled in here, get the locks changed, get my own things out of storage, all that kind of stuff and be on the plane to Amsterdam Tuesday morning."

"Good heavens. Amsterdam?"

She nodded. "You said I didn't look like an ex-circus performer. Actually, I'm not an ex. I *am* a circus performer. I'm part of a high wire act and at the moment we're with a German troupe out of Bonn. We open in Amsterdam next Thursday for a two-week run. Now, what did you want to ask me about Dian?"

"Anything you can tell me. But first, I'd better tell you why I'm asking." I explained about Birdie, and Rosellen, and then went on. "How close were you to Dian? She was supposedly Howard's mistress. Did she ever talk to you about him?"

"Yes, and no. That is, I knew she was seeing him, but I didn't think it was anything that serious. She couldn't have known him long. I was as surprised as everyone else when the bodies were found together."

"She must have been missing, or at least not at the place you shared, for some time. Didn't you wonder where she was?"

"Again, yes and no. She had been talking about quitting for a month or more. Circus life is neither as glamorous nor as easy as it looks. She wasn't born to it as I was and she was getting tired of the hard work involved. She didn't use the room we shared all that much but when she missed a couple of performances I simply thought she had taken off for greener pastures. We'd been there, based in Everett and Bellingham, for nearly two months and were due to leave for Idaho a few days after the bodies were found. I just figured she didn't want to go."

"One of the police reports said she was thirty. Was that right?"

She frowned. "I thought she was older than that. She seemed like it to me, but I was only sixteen then so anyone over twenty-five was old to me."

"The police did question you about her, didn't they?"

"No. They didn't. They talked to Freddie, he managed the acts, but they never asked me or anyone else a thing. Someone came and took all her stuff away but even he didn't ask anything, and a lot of her things were missing. I knew because I'd packed up what she'd left behind when I decided she wasn't coming back. A week or so before we heard what happened. To tell the truth, I thought it was darned strange. I still do."

I thought it was a whole lot more than just strange.

Chapter Twenty-four

I stopped at a Thai place on Broadway to eat on the way back so it was after five when I got to the office. Martha was gone but she had left a stack of mail, a couple of telephone messages, and an e-mail printout on my desk. The e-mail was from my Denver friend, Ted Kettle, regarding the diary pages I'd faxed him. It was brief and to the point, saying:

Hi:
  I put those pages thru every decoding analysis I have and I sent them on to my contact in Langley, too. We both agree. It's a personal code and without having a clearer copy of the original there is no way to unravel it. And not very likely even then. Sorry.

Ted

The telephone messages were from Captain Nordan and from Sam, both asking me to call back. I threw them in the trash.

I thought about going home and crawling into bed but despite feeling rotten—I'd had no sleep the night before, unless you could call passing out on the beach sleep—my brain was in overdrive trying to make sense of all I'd seen or heard in the last forty-eight hours. I wanted to get it all into the computer where I could sort things into some kind of order. So much of what I'd learned about Howard Swallow's death contradicted itself.

Birdie said there was no evidence that her grandfather went to San Francisco, nor that he had ever planned to do so. Berthe saw him packing a suitcase the Monday after Memorial Day. If he wasn't going to San Francisco where was he going? Who was right? Or, who was lying?

"Maybe he was going to run off with Dian," I muttered.

Cyndie said many of Dian's clothes were gone from their room at about the same time but no one had questioned her about them. No one had questioned her at all. Why not? She was Dian's roommate and in the normal course of things she should have been interviewed by the detective in charge. Leon Kieski.

Why were neither one of these details included in any of Kieski's reports?

Olin Peterson said a man who claimed to be Howard Swallow called the bank on or about the 15th of the month, two days before the bodies were found. He reported the conversation to Captain Clinton who was in charge of the case but he never heard anything further about it. No one ever interviewed him either. Why not? Why was the only mention of Peterson a penciled notation in the margin of a note about something else entirely?

Looking at what I'd written about Peterson suddenly

reminded me of something Birdie had said the afternoon before the birthday party. She said Rosellen was an accomplished actress. She could sound like anyone, *and so could Howard*. Had he been the one who called the bank in an effort to confuse the time of his father's death? And if so, why?

I sat and thought about that for a few minutes. *Que bono?* Who gains? If anyone gained it was Howard. He was, and had been for twenty-two years, in total control of the Swallow estate. What I needed to do next was find out exactly what that estate was worth, and if he was actually a court-appointed trustee. Martha hadn't been able to find any record of him being appointed anything, but maybe I could find out by simply asking him. Not that he would necessarily tell me, or even answer me at all, but on the other hand, why shouldn't he? I was supposedly working for his niece. And however he responded it might give me a clue.

I reached for the telephone and then decided to call Birdie instead. She didn't answer so I left a message on her answering machine. She might know or she could ask her mother. I could always call Howard tomorrow.

I went on keyboarding in my talks with Berthe Anderson and with Cyndie Dancer.

Last night both Jake and I had read and reread the stuff he'd copied—he'd made two copies of everything, one for himself—but we found no mention of the pearl-handled gun. Not even a reference to unspecified physical evidence. What had happened to it? And was it still around somewhere?

Another thing that had struck me as being off-center somehow was the blood-stained spread that had been found buried on the beach. As far as I could tell from reading Kieski's notes there hadn't been any attempt to clean up the cabin, so why had the killer tried to hide the spread? Because Howard and Dian had been lying on it? They had been lying on the mattress too but nothing had been done with it.

Or was the entire setup in the cabin phony? Had they been killed on the beach and the blood spots in the cabin been simply window dressing? For all any official reports said to the contrary they could have been chicken blood. Was that why there hadn't been any record of DNA testing?

And no matter where they had been killed how had the two bodies gotten from the cabin into the freezer? That was another little item that hadn't been addressed in any of the police reports. And why hadn't the killer dumped the bodies in the Sound where I'd been knocked in? Unconscious, the tide would have carried them out and they would probably never have been found. The marine creatures would have taken care of that.

It was after ten before I gave up and went home. I still had more questions than I had answers but I was beginning to believe Birdie was right. Someone had railroaded her Gran into Windsor House.

I woke the next morning feeling worse than the day before. I'd apparently used every muscle in my body struggling toward the beach and from the way some of them were feeling it was the first time they had been used in a long time. A hot shower and aspirin helped some but not enough to more than just take the edge off the aches and pains, or my increasingly angry thinking.

To start with when I got home I'd found a message on my answering machine from Captain Nordan. I do have a short fuse but most of the time I am, as the saying goes, just full of sound and fury quickly gone. Not this time. I was mad clear through. I didn't like Captain Nordan's tone, I didn't believe in the bear, and I was more than ever sure that someone had not only had Rosellen imprisoned for something she hadn't done, that same person had tried to stop me from finding out what had really happened back then.

"And murdered Ruth because she was about to tell someone, maybe even me."

The sound of my voice startled me. I hadn't realized I was thinking aloud, nor that the idea was in my head even, but I was suddenly sure it was the real reason for her death. Nothing else fit, and there was something about all three killings that was constant, that had the same feel. I just couldn't tie enough pieces together to get a fix on what it was.

I started to get dressed to go to the office before I remembered it was Saturday. Birdie still hadn't returned my call and I probably wouldn't be able to contact anyone else I wanted to talk to either so I might as well take the weekend off and go up to my friend Sherry's horse ranch north of Monroe. I was always welcome there. I needed time to recover from Thursday night's near catastrophe and maybe the peace and quiet of her place would clear my mind. The whole Swallow situation was so muddled, so full of inconsistencies I couldn't get a handle on any of it. A throbbing headache wasn't helping, either.

With that settled I threw a few clothes in an overnight bag, put on a T-shirt, a pair of jeans, and a lightweight madras jacket that was a size too large for me. It was loose enough to conceal the back-belt holster and the .32 I dug out of its hiding place. I don't like guns and very rarely ever carry one around but I intended to do so from now on. Or at least until I figured out who was responsible for the three murders. I didn't intend to be the fourth victim if I could help it and somebody obviously thought I was getting close to finding the answers.

It was too bad I didn't know what it was I was getting close to.

Chapter Twenty-five

I was driving home, on my way to the office Monday morning, when I had another thought about Howard and the estate. I might have been looking for more than had been needed.

Regardless of whether her family thought her guilty or not, Rosellen had not been tried for Howard's murder. In the eyes of the law she was innocent, so, in the absence of a will to the contrary, she had inherited the Swallow estate.

I'd have Martha search the records but I had a feeling no will had ever been probated. All Howard needed was Rosellen's power of attorney. And she had more than likely signed those papers too when she had signed herself into Windsor House.

The weekend at Sherry's place, high blue skies, towering mountains, and the simple pleasure of watching beautiful horses in white-fenced pastures, had restored my sore muscles and unkinked some of my thinking. The power of attorney was just one of the ideas that had surfaced.

I went looking for Anna as soon as I got to the office and asked her if such a document would give Junior the authority to do anything he wanted.

"Sure. Why not?" she said, shrugging. "All that would be needed was the correct paperwork, two witnesses and a notary."

"A power of attorney doesn't have to be recorded?"

"Nope. And it's good forever. It's hard to rescind too. Which is one of the reasons I never recommend one except for specific limited use. Or time. A power of attorney is as good as your own signature. Good for anything, although Howard might run into a little trouble when he sells the house, depends on the title. Didn't you say you had asked someone to do a title search for you?"

"Yes, Penny Sawyer."

"Well, when you get it bring it over. I'd like to see how it's worded."

I was wrong about the will. One had been entered for probate the week after Rosellen went into Windsor. It was a simple two-page document leaving everything to Rosellen. One of Martha's e-mail pals visited the county court house, found it without any problem and faxed the lot to her before noon. Everything had been recorded in Snohomish County and from the looks of the dates on the relevant papers it had been pushed through the system at a much faster rate than was usual.

"With one thing and another, including this bit, I think I'd start wondering if Howard is quite the loving son he claims to be," Martha said, nodding at the sheaf of faxes she had handed me.

"H-mm. Does make one speculate a bit, doesn't it," I said, flipping through the pages. I thought a minute. "There is no way of proving, or disproving, where anyone was when Howard and Dian were killed. It was too long ago and as far as I can tell there isn't even a tentative time of death on record."

"So?"

"That isn't true of Ruth's murder. We know pretty much when it happened. Jane's mother saw someone on Ruth's porch at ten of twelve Monday night. She thought it was Ruth so she didn't pay any attention and doesn't know whether the figure was going in or coming out but it's a good bet it was the killer leaving. So I can start from there. Where was everyone at midnight?"

"You're thinking they are connected? That the motive reaches from Howard and Dian to Ruth? Twenty-two years? That's quite a stretch, Demary. Have you got any reason, anything at all to connect them?"

"Well, yes and no, but there is one possibility." I repeated the scrap of conversation I'd overheard in the hall that night between Ruth and Howard. "Ruth knew something and I'm thinking the killer had reason to suppose she was going to tell what she knew. Maybe she told him so."

"Pretty thin," she said, frowning. "It might give Howard a motive, maybe, but from what Sam told you he's in the clear."

"True, but she could have talked to one of the others, too. Whatever is going on, or has gone on, I think they all know about it. Or at least the three siblings do. Howard, Dorothy, and Alison. I'd like to know where all of them were the night Ruth died."

"Have you asked Sam?"

"No, will you call him for me? Find out if he has—"

"No, I won't," she said sharply. "I'm not getting in the middle of one of your battles. If you want to talk to the man you—"

"I can't, Martha. I'm too mad at him. If I talk to—"

"No, I won't do it. In the first place you have no business being mad at him at all. He has a perfect right to take someone besides you out to dinner. So do your own dirty work."

With that she turned and strode out of the room, her lemon-colored skirt swishing with disapproval.

I glared at her retreating back. She was right, of course. I had no right to be mad at Sam. Which didn't change a thing. I'd just have to get along with any help from the Homicide department.

On the other hand, Carol Ann was in Homicide. I could call her.

"I don't know anything about the case," she said when I finally got her on the line a couple of hours later. "I'm working something else. Ask Sam."

"Uh, no. I don't want to ask him."

"Why not? Are you two feuding again? Honestly, Demary. Why don't you either get married or give up? The both of you are a pain. And besides that, now that I think about it, you've got no business messing in an ongoing murder investigation and you know it."

"Please, Carol Ann. I can't ask him. Just see what you can find out, will you?"

"Oh, all right, I'll try, but I wish you guys would make up your minds what you want."

With that she slammed her phone down. I gritted my teeth and went back to working on a list of everyone who was present at the Swallow house the two weeks surrounding Howard's death, what I knew of their relationships and where they had been, or might have been, the night of Ruth's murder.

Their whereabouts the night of Ruth's murder were mostly speculation but getting it down on paper—or in this case on the screen—let me get it straight in my mind. There were eight family members with a possible motive for getting rid of Ruth. I was guessing, of course, but I felt certain the motive for her death was connected to Howard and Dian's death and to Rosellen's incarceration in Windsor House. Of those eight people, however, only four were present at the time and old enough to have had anything to do with the earlier murders. Birdie's mother Dorothy, Junior, Alison, and Jordan. Which didn't mean one of the younger ones hadn't done Ruth in. Either to protect their parents or on their own hook to protect their source of income. The first three were the most likely suspects, however.

I knew that Junior had an alibi even if it wasn't airtight but I didn't know about the others. Jordan had been home, alone. I'd asked him straight out Friday morning while I was eating peaches and toast, and told him why I wanted to know. Probably not the best idea I'd ever had but at the time I was so stressed from the previous night's adventure I hadn't been thinking too straight.

The question hadn't seemed to disturb him though. He answered willingly enough and told me that although he couldn't prove where he was at midnight he could prove he was at home at nine-forty-five. A friend had called him and he'd give me the name if I wanted it. I didn't bother. His house was less than a half hour from Ruth's so he'd had plenty of time to be on her porch at ten to twelve if he was guilty.

I was counting on Birdie to give me an idea of where her mother was but she still hadn't answered my message. Actually two messages as I'd called her again from Sherry's early that morning.

That left Alison, and her husband George. To my mind both were very unlikely suspects for Ruth's murder but that didn't mean they didn't know what was going on. They lived in Gig Harbor where George owned and operated a small nursery that specialized in growing herbs that he packaged and sold to supermarkets all over western Washington. George had never known Howard. He and Alison hadn't met until after her father was gone.

I looked up their number and called.

To my surprise Birdie answered the phone.

"Birdie? What in the world are you doing down there?" I asked after identifying myself.

"Trying to help," she said in a strained voice. "Mom's here too. There isn't much we can do though. We've been trying to keep the nursery going as best as we can but without Uncle George it's pretty hard. It's all just too terrible."

"What is, Birdie? Tell me. What's happened? Is George sick? Dead? What?"

"No. No. It's Jane. Jane was run down by a hit and run driver last Monday. And we didn't even find out about it for two days. She was in the hospital, unconscious, for two days before they found out who she was."

Jane was Alison and George's only child.

"Oh, Birdie, I'm so sorry," I said. "I know you were good friends. Is she going to be all right?"

"The doctors don't know," she said, crying now. "They still can't tell. They . . . they think she may have some brain damage. And Demary, it happened right in our own neighborhood. On Stoneway over near where you turn to go up on the bridge."

My mind flipped into high gear. "When, Birdie? When?"

"Monday. I told you. A little after midnight."

Minutes after her Aunt Ruth had been killed. I wondered what the odds would be on the two deaths being unrelated.

Chapter Twenty-six

It took a while, with two incoherent stops and a lot of tears, but eventually I was pretty sure I understood what had happened. Jane, who is working on her Master's degree at the University of Washington, had gone to a friend's apartment a half block off Stoneway to borrow notes on a lecture she had missed. While there another friend, a young man, had arrived and all three of them had walked several blocks down the street to a tavern.

At approximately eleven-thirty Jane's friend, Linda, and the young man went back to her apartment, leaving Jane talking with other friends. About a half hour later she left to go back to her car. As she started across the intersection of Ashworth and North 41st she was hit by what the police thought was a stolen car that had since been found parked on a side street a few blocks away. Fortunately another motorist coming from the opposite direction had seen what happened and immediately called 911.

Jane had left her purse locked in her car and had nothing in her pockets except her car keys and two dollar bills so it had taken some time to identify her. In the meantime neither her friends nor family had any idea anything had happened to her.

She was now, nearly a week later, still in a semiconscious condition. Plus the doctors were keeping her heavily sedated so no one had been able to talk to her yet.

"And we were all right there, too," Birdie wailed. "But we didn't know a thing."

I frowned. "What do you mean, you were all right there?"

"We were all right there in the neighborhood. I was home, of course, but Aunt Alison and George and Mom were playing cards. Right while it was happening," she sobbed. "They were staying overnight with Mom. George had a dentist's appointment that afternoon. They always stay with Mom when they come up to Seattle."

"And the next morning you found out about Ruth."

"Yes-s-s. It's be-been really awful," she said, hiccupping.

We continued to talk for a few minutes and when we hung up she had at calmed down enough to quit crying but she was still very upset. I didn't blame her. To have two such catastrophes at one time was overwhelming and I knew she was fond of both the victims.

My list of possible suspects for Ruth's murder was still up on the computer screen when I put the phone down. Looking at it almost made me laugh. Sam was right—I would be well advised to stick to genealogy. I was certainly a washout as a detective. With the possible exception of Jordan all my so-called suspects had excellent alibis. And as he had an iron-clad alibi for Howard and Dian's murders I couldn't see that he had any motive for Ruth's.

I sighed and reached for the phone again. Martha was

right, too. I had no business being mad at Sam, and he
needed to know about Jane. He might know already of
course, but it wasn't likely. No one working hit-run
would have any reason to associate Jane Davis with Ruth
Swallow.

I decided the easiest way to go was to start with an
apology and did so the minute he got on the phone.

"I'm sorry I was such an idiot the other morning," I
said. "My only excuse is that I wasn't over the shock of
being thrown in the Sound."

"Uh, yes. So I figured," he said cautiously. "Are you
okay now? No after-effects?"

"I'm fine. I spent the weekend up at Sherry's. That's
always good therapy. I'll tell you about being at the
Swallow place if you want but that isn't why I called.
Has anyone told you about Jane Davis?"

"No, who is . . . Oh, yes. Alison and George Davis's
daughter. What about her?"

I told him.

He asked a couple of questions and then said, "It
might not have any connection to the Swallow killing,
but whether it does or not it is one whale of a coincidence."

"How do you mean?"

"Think about it. It could have been an unrelated accident, or, whoever was driving was waiting for her specifically, or, it was Ruth's killer and he had the bad luck
to be at that corner the same exact moment she was and
she recognized him. Or her. In any case it was some
coincidence. They do happen though."

He was right. Regardless of how it happened, or why,
it was eerie.

"Demary, I'll ask you again, stay out of it," he went
on in a quietly deliberate voice. "I mean it this time when

I say I'll bring charges against you if I have to. You must stay out of this one. You hear me?"

I started to tell him to stick it in his ear but stopped myself in time. I didn't want to get into another fight with him. That didn't mean I couldn't keep working on Howard and Dian's death. And if I found the connection, well, I found it. So I agreed in as meek a voice as I could manage and we hung up.

I hadn't asked him about his dinner date, and I knew I never would. I had, belatedly, realized that our relationship, as precarious and rocky as it was, meant a lot to me.

I had no sooner put the phone down than Carol Ann called.

"I found out some stuff for you but I can't talk right now," she said quickly. "I'll meet you at the Cornerpost for dinner. That place over near Sherry's apartment. I've got to come back to the office after. Six-thirty, maybe seven? Okay?"

I agreed and we rang off.

Martha was already packing up to leave for the day so I decided to knock off early, too. It was a few minutes after four.

Joey came skateboarding down the sidewalk just as I pulled into my driveway. He rolled to a fancy stop beside the Toyota and came over to the window before I could get out.

"You ever see that place Buddy's grandmother is in?" he asked, scratching his stomach. His shirt was so tight it looked like it was glued on him. A pair of dolphins painted on the front of it frolicked in the waves as he breathed. Or at least I hoped that was what they were doing.

"Windsor House? No. How do you know where she is?"

"Buddy told Janay about it. His dad took him over there a couple of times. Jimmy Carmichael and I checked it out this afternoon."

"You what? How did you get up there?"

"Up where? It's only over in Ballard. We took the bus. Didn't try to go in, couldn't figured out what kind of a story to use. But we did take a good look around. For a nuthouse it's sure a loose caboose."

I was too surprised at the location to ask what he thought he was doing. No one had ever said so but I'd supposed Windsor to be in Everett.

"Are you sure it's the right place?" I asked.

"Yep. Big place. Looks like it used to be some kind of a mansion. Been built on to some, too. Lots of grass and trees and stuff around it. Lots of doors too. A wonder half their nuts don't wander off on them."

I glanced at my watch. I had plenty of time. "You want to show me where it is?"

"Sure." He vaulted over the fender and came around to the passenger side. "Go straight over to 15th and up to 81st. I'll tell you from there."

I did as he said and in due course we stopped in front of what looked like, as he'd said, an old nineteenth-century mansion set in a block-wide expanse of lawn and gardens. A small brass plate set into the cornerpost of the low brick fence that encircled the place bore the name and street number. Built of big blocks of gray granite, it had a heavy look that was lightened by a wide covered porch across the entire front crowded with chairs and lounges sporting brightly colored cushions. A number of older people, both men and women, dressed in conventional summer clothes were sitting in the chairs or walking slowly back and forth along the porch railing. Three younger women and two men, wearing what looked more like uniforms, were also present.

"Were there people out on the porch when you were here before?" I asked.

"Yep. You watch you see none of them gets off the porch though. Those two guys in the uniforms stay by the steps to see they don't. Saw one of old birds try it. Around back they can go down on the grass but there's a high fence around that part."

I watched for a while and then asked, "You said they could wander off. How?"

"Big old place like this there's a dozen doors. I don't know what the setup is inside but we tried a couple of them and they weren't locked. One of them we tried looked like it led down into the basement. It isn't ten feet from the street at the back of the place. Some of those old geezers look pretty spry to me. They could walk away easy."

Chapter Twenty-seven

I dropped Joey off at home and went on over to the Cornerpost without bothering to go home myself. I'd be a little early but I could use a some thinking time. (As it happened, I got caught in a backup of traffic on Mercer and was a few minutes late.)

I knew Joey was wrong about the security at Windsor. He might have found some outside doors unlocked all right, probably for the convenience of the staff, but you could be sure the residents didn't have any access to the exits. Many of their patients would be suffering from Alzheimer's disease so they would be very careful about security. Alzheimer's patients are notorious wanderers. What puzzled me was what Rosellen was doing there. I could be wrong, of course, but it didn't seem to be much more than a secure health-care facility. It certainly didn't appear to be a psychiatric institution.

If the authorities were so sure Rosellen was guilty of a double murder why would they agree to drop prosecution simply because she was confined in what looked like fairly luxurious quarters? It didn't make sense. Not from a legal point of view.

I made myself a mental note to find out more about Windsor House. A lot more.

Carol Ann was already at a table when I got to the Cornerpost. She looked tired and cross, which was un- usual for her. She has the most laid-back personality of anyone I know.

"Hi, Demary," she said as I sat. "I'm having a glass of white wine. Want one?"

"Sure."

"You know, I think Sam's right," she said after the waitress had deposited my wine and taken our orders. "Whenever you get into a case it gets twice as complicated."

"Wha-a-t?" I gasped, preparing to do battle.

She waved her hand negligently. "Oh, I don't suppose it's your fault. Exactly. But there I was, minding my own business, checking out a simple hit-run, when all of a sudden I'm right in the middle of the blasted Swallow case."

"You were working the Davis hit-run?" Talk about coincidence!

"Well, yes and no. I was checking out the owner of the car who happens to have a sheet as long as your arm."

"Good grief."

"H-m-m, yes. We don't have all that many homicides going at the moment so I got the job of making sure the guy was where he said he was when the Davis girl got hit."

"Was he?"

Nodding, she said, "He not only was where he said he was, a bar out in the north end, he was talking to a couple of black and whites who were nearby and got the call when he'd reported the car stolen an hour before." She laughed. "And what is really funny is that he has been hauled in a half dozen times for that very thing. Car theft."

"So why are you so bent out of shape? And how does it get to be my fault?"

"I just told you. We don't have much to do right now but instead of me getting a couple of easy days for a change the minute you tied the hit-run to the murder I drew the job of correlating the whole schmeer. And you know what that means. A ton of paperwork even on the computer."

Carol Ann hated paperwork. I didn't, however, offer sympathy. If she was correlating reports it meant she could really keep me up to date. And I knew she would. Carol Ann is as casual as Jake when it comes to departmental information. Which she more than proved as we ate.

We had both ordered a half-size Cobb salad. They were delicious, chock full of crumbled bacon, sliced avocado, and strips of grilled chicken breast, but so huge I wondered who could possibly eat a full-sized one.

"It doesn't seem too likely but it could be a coincidence, you know," I said, taking a bite of avocado. "Guy steals a car, has a couple of drinks, goes joy-riding around, and whammo, he hits a pedestrian."

"Joy-riding around the back streets? Ten miles from where he lifted the car? Don't give me that!" She gave an unladylike snort. "Even if we didn't have a witness I wouldn't believe it. No, he hit her deliberately and the most likely reason is because he had just come from the Swallow house and she recognized him."

"The witness is sure it was deliberate?"

"Well, you judge. The two cars were on Ashworth. The witness, Adam Green, fifty-six years old, was driving north. Hit-run south, on the same side of the street as the girl as she got to the intersection. According to Green neither car was going over ten miles an hour as they approached the corner. He was still about fifty feet from the crosswalk when the other car came to a full stop. There are two good street lights at that intersection, plus headlights from both cars, so the scene was not only clear to both drivers—when Davis got to the corner she must have been able to see the driver of the hit-run, too. Green had slowed to a crawl when she reached the curb diagonally across from him. She glanced at him, the hit-run was already stopped, remember, looked at it, and started to cross, which put her directly in front of the hit-run car. It accelerated, knocking her sideways and into the gutter on the other side of the street, then wheeled around the corner and was gone before Green realized what had happened."

"Deliberate then."

"Very."

"Any doubts about Green's story?"

She shook her head. "No. He was positive about what he saw and the physical evidence bears him out. No reason to lie either."

"You said, or he said, Jane looked first at him and then at the other driver as she stepped off the curb. Did she show any sign of recognizing the other driver?"

"He couldn't say one way or the other. In his opinion she looked at him first to make sure he wasn't coming on across the intersection, then just glanced at the other car as she started across. It was already stopped so it wouldn't, to her mind, represent any danger. My guess is that was when she recognized the driver, he saw she did, panicked and hit the accelerator."

I nodded. "Must have happened fast. Minute or less. Green remembered a lot for anything that happened so quickly."

"Not really. Seeing the other car, the girl, slowing down, the relative positions, that was all automatic. The only atypical thing he noticed was that she looked at him first, then the other car, and even that wasn't particularly unusual in the circumstances."

We had come to the end of our salads, or what we could finish anyway, and waited until the waitress had removed the plates and poured coffee before we went back to the Swallow case.

"What was the exact time?" I asked. "The 911 operator must have logged it."

"Seventeen minutes after twelve."

"So if Mrs. Hollie, Janay's mother, is right about the time she saw the figure on Ruth's back porch we have about twenty-five minutes of the killer's time unaccounted for. It's about six blocks from Bagley to Ashworth. Five minutes at the most including getting to his car."

"If he drove straight over there. Which he didn't because he was headed in the wrong direction to have come directly from her house. Bagley is east of Ashworth. Both streets run north-south. So he went somewhere else first."

I thought about Birdie and her parents, both living within a mile's range of Ruth's house. Could the killer have been checking on one of them? And with what in mind?

I shook my head in frustration. No point in following

that line of thought, unless the killer was intent on wiping out the whole family.

I passed the idea on to Carol Ann.

"Why?" she asked. "I mean what possible motive would tie the family together in anyone's mind? Carl Wilson interviewed all of them and according to his reports most of them don't even seem to like each other, let alone have enough in common to give anyone else a collective motive. Last week, Rosellen Swallow's birthday, was the first time they had all been together at the family home in over five years. Sam is nothing if not thorough. You know that. And even then, last week, they weren't all there. Jane wasn't."

"How about Howard and Dian's murder?"

"How about . . . ? How about what? That was twenty-two years ago. Alison Swallow was still in school, Ruth Swallow hadn't even met Junior, and Jane wasn't born. Sam talked to the DA's office in Snohomish. He wasn't around at the time but says the surviving files are definite about Rosellen's guilt. She was unable to stand trial, however, and was put away."

"Surviving files?"

"H-m-m, yes. They had a fire in the courthouse a couple of years after Howard's death and lost most of the paperwork involved."

Well, well, I thought. *Now isn't that interesting.* The police reports were incomplete and the normally secure files from the DA's office were at least partly missing. Coincidence again?

My foot. Fires do happen but coincidence would only stretch so far and there were too many coincidences in this case to qualify as such.

There was a guiding hand somewhere. One that had

been active for a long time. One of the family? It seemed like it had to be, but which one?

Or was I going at the problem from the wrong angle? Could it be someone in the DA's office? The judge? One of the investigating officers? Kieski himself? Someone who was trying to bury a massive error?

The idea fit Ruth's comment in the hall that night, and I didn't know anything to contradicted the thought. It opened up a whole new field. When it came to motive there was nothing like trying to conceal a big mistake. Particularly if the mistake had to do with a double murder.

Chapter Twenty-eight

My answering machine light was sparkling merrily when I got home. I had messages from Captain Nordan, Birdie, Martha, Penny Sawyer, and Jordan Wyndlow.

I called Jordan first.

"How are you feeling now?" Jordan asked after I identified myself.

"Much better. In fact, other than still being a little black and blue, I'm fine," I told him, wondering why he'd called. He was still on my mental list of suspects.

"Good. I thought I'd let you know the wildlife service captured your assailant this morning. The poor thing was hungry. She was rooting around in a Dumpster in broad daylight. Both she and her two cubs are on their way to a more suitable home in the mountains."

"It really was a bear?" I asked, somewhat stupidly.

"Yes. A small black bear. We get them around here quite frequently. They swim across from Whidby Island." I could hear the smile in his voice. "Not, as I'm sure you thought, a wandering maniac."

I hadn't thought anything of the kind and he knew it but I wasn't about to tell him what I had thought.

"Well, thanks for telling me about it, uh, her. I'm strictly a city girl and I guess the idea of a bear practically right in town just seemed too impossible for me to take in. And thanks again for rescuing me, too."

"No problem. Any time," he said agreeably as we rang off.

Birdie was next. She was at home, still weepy, and wanted me to accompany her to Windsor the next morning to see Rosellen.

"The doctor called this evening. Called Aunt Alison really but I answered the phone. He wanted to talk to a member of the family, so I said I'd come tomorrow morning. Please come with me, Demary."

"Yes, all right, I'll go but why doesn't your mother go? Or Howard? They're the eldest," I said.

"Because I didn't tell her. She is so worried about Jane, and trying to keep the nursery going for Alison and George, she's about exhausted. I'll see what the doctor wants. Mom just can't take much more. George is supposed to be back tomorrow though. At least for the day. The doctors say Jane is doing better this evening. They've taken her off the critical list."

I thought briefly of telling her what Carol Ann had told me about the accident but dismissed the idea before it was half formed. She didn't need any additional aggro.

My next call was to Penny.

"Hi, Demary. I faxed you the title search on the Swallow place around five, before I saw it on multiple-listing. Thought I'd let you know tonight because it's going to go fast. Good price," she said.

For a moment I couldn't imagine what she was talking about, then it dawned on me.

"Good heavens, Penny. I'm not interested in buying it. I told you, or thought I did, that I wanted to know in connection with a case I'm working on."

"Oh, uh, yes, you did, but I thought . . ." She laughed. "Okay. I'm sorry. I should have known better. You would have told me straight up if you were interested in a purchase. It's just that so many people . . . Never mind. What did you need to know about it anyway?"

"Who holds the title and is it free and clear?"

"The property was quit-claimed to Howard Martindale Swallow IV in June, twenty, uh . . . twenty-two years ago. Taxes have been paid to date, there are no assessments and no liens."

That took care of that.

Martha had Captain Nordan on her mind.

"Demary, please call him. He called me here at home this evening. I don't know how he got my number."

"Out of the phone book."

"Oh, yes, I suppose so. Anyway, I think we were wrong about him. He wasn't being rude the other day. He's a sick man. He was calling from Providence Hospital." She went on to give me the telephone and his room number.

"Do you know what's wrong with him?" I asked.

"No. I didn't like to ask. He had apparently tried to get you and when he couldn't he called me. He wanted to make sure you didn't make the Alaska trip until we heard from him again. Something must be very wrong."

I glanced at my watch. "It's too late to call tonight. But I'll do it first thing in the morning."

I had just hung up when the phone rang. It was Jake.

"I think I've found out why Kieski had you followed

the other day," he said cheerfully. "It's been bothering me so I asked a few questions. He still has a reputation around here of being pretty rough and of skating too close to the edge. I think he wanted to make sure you weren't working undercover for the department. He wanted to make sure you didn't head straight for the cop-shop when you left his place."

"What? Why in the world . . . What would give him that idea?"

"Paranoia. It's a long story. I found out the property clerk in the Everett P.D. is an old hand so I bought him a couple of beers and he told me all about it. He, Larry Wilson, was a rookie when Howard and Dian were killed and although he didn't have anything to do with the investigation he knew a lot about what happened. Including the fact that Kieski was called on the carpet for his handling of the case, and, in fact, there was talk of an I.A. investigation."

"Wow." I.A. was Internal Affairs. They investigated possible malfeasance on the part of any officer regardless of rank. No wonder Kieski had been so belligerent on the subject.

"Right. And that ain't all, baby," Jake said, mocking a current TV police show. "Kieski's wife had divorced him about six months before that and according to the gossip had cleaned him out. Taken everything they owned. But, six months after Swallow's death he bought himself a new house. The one where you saw him. He claimed to have gotten a big inheritance from an uncle no one had ever heard him mention before."

"Possible, I guess."

"Yep. Possible, but opinion at the time said payoff. Loud and clear. In fact, according to Larry, the whole case smelled of payola."

So maybe that was where the missing money had gone. Not into a hidden bank account, into hidden pockets. "Who was getting paid for what? Did he know?" I asked.

"Nope. He doesn't remember much about the investigation itself, says he never knew much, what he remembers is the gossip that was floating around."

"Did you run the plate of the blue Ford?"

"Oh. Yes. I forgot. It's a state car. Out of the motor pool in Bellingham, and Kieski's sister is married to a state trooper. So . . ."

I was silent for a moment. "Why in the world would Kieski think I was working for the Everett P.D.?" I asked finally. "Martha made the appointment and made it clear why I wanted to talk to him. Plus, unless he killed Howard and Dian, whatever he did or didn't do is water under the bridge now. If nothing else, the statue of limitations would exempt him from prosecution."

"Beats me. Like I said, paranoia."

We kicked it around for a while longer before we hung up but came to no conclusions. None that made any sense anyway, but talking to him did make me decide I didn't want to even think about the Swallow case any more. Everything I learned just seemed to make it more complicated. I needed to think about something else so I carried the stack of stuff on the Kalakala I'd brought home upstairs with me and set it on my bedside table before I got my nightgown out. The thinnest one I had. It had been unseasonably hot all day and I don't have any air-conditioning so my bedroom was warm and stuffy. Even with the windows wide open I knew I'd have a hard time getting to sleep. Reading about the old ferry might be better than counting sheep.

I went back downstairs for some sustenance to see me

through the pile: an ice-cold cola, a sack of salt/lime potato chips, and a plate of thin-sliced hard salami. It's no wonder I'm at least ten pounds overweight again.

Much of what I read I'd seen before. Some had been printed recently and concerned the restoration project, but as I sifted through the pile I discovered several things that had been written years ago while the beautiful streamlined boat had still been plying the waters of Puget Sound.

One of which was the little hardcover book, *The Silver Beauty*. It was well written but so full of facts and figures I thought it would surely send me off into slumberland.

It did the opposite. It not only woke me wide awake, it sent me jumping out of bed with an excited gasp.

The big ferry, built in 1925 and named the *Peralta*, had been put into service for the Key Transit Company in San Francisco Bay where it operated for nearly ten years. In 1933, the same year prohibition was repealed by the Twenty-first Amendment, it was purchased by the Puget Sound Navigation Company and towed to Seattle where it was to be rebuilt and renamed the *Kalakala*.

At that point in the narrative the writer switched subjects and began talking about the various vessels that had run booze from the many coves and islands off the Canadian coast to the U.S. mainland. He not only gave details of how it was done, he named many of the skippers and their boats, with descriptions, including tonnage.

One of the boats he mentioned was named the Rossleven, a converted deep-water tug, captained by Howard Swallow, known more familiarly as "Birdie."

I nearly fell down the last few steps to the hall where I rushed into my office and grabbed Rosellen's so-called diary off my desk where I'd left it the week before.

One look was all it took. The faded and blurred name on the first page wasn't Rosellen, it was Rossleven. The first line I'd read, "J2 s12c ch5c og," and couldn't understand, was clear as a Waterford goblet now. It reminded Captain Swallow that on June or July second he had transported twelve cases of scotch, five cases of champagne, and zero cases of gin from Canada to his front beach.

Birdie, my Birdie, would no doubt be horrified, but I loved it.

Chapter Twenty-nine

I got up early the next day. The morning was still cool and fresh when I got to the office. I was full of ideas. They were swirling through my head like confetti and I wanted to get them into the computer before the details got away from me. Regardless of whether he was guilty or not, thinking about who could have bribed Kieski had led me straight back to Junior. All things considered I doubted that Kieski would have dealt with a woman and the only two males in the family available at the time were Jordan and Junior. Dorothy's husband had been killed in Vietnam and Alison hadn't yet met George.

Jordan was certainly a possibility but to my mind he was unlikely. With his record and having just been arrested the way he was I didn't think Kieski—or anyone else—would have trusted him.

On the other hand Junior was a member of the bar, worked for a prestigious firm and was in a position to bring pressure to bear in a number of places. Plus he had the money, which Jordan did not. Junior had been the one who did all the wheeling and dealing that had been done. He was the one Rosellen had quit-claimed the property to, he had shepherded her through the court and into Windsor House. And he was the one who continued to handle the finances.

He was also the one who was the deepest in debt.

There was no way I could prove he had killed Howard and Dian, although I did think I could prove some involvement. I made a note to have Martha find out where Cyndie Dancer's circus was and to send her a picture of Junior. I wanted to know if he was the man who had picked up Dian's clothes. And I wanted to talk to Berthe Anderson again too. I wanted to know, specifically, how Junior had behaved toward her. Particularly if he'd been as arrogant as the others.

What I did think I might be able to prove was that he had killed Ruth, and tried to kill Jane. Thinking about Jane led me to wonder if Sam had posted a guard on her. If she regained consciousness she'd be able to name the driver. Without thinking, I called Sam at home to ask him about her security.

To my shock a woman answered. A young woman. For a moment I was too stunned to even hang up. Fortunately that didn't last beyond her second "Hello." I replaced my phone carefully, stared at the wall for a few minutes, and went back to work on the computer. I was not going to let any thoughts of who she was or what she was doing in Sam's house at that hour of the morning keep me from proving that Howard Martindale Swallow IV had murdered his aunt and tried to kill his niece.

Martha came to work at nine. I caught her up on what Jake and Carol Ann had told me, told her what I'd found out about the "diary" and what I thought about Howard Junior. She was delighted about the diary, and also thought it was funny, but very dubious about Junior.

"He was in Vancouver, Demary. He couldn't have driven down here in time and if he hired someone to off Ruth how would Jane have recognized him?"

"We have a new means of getting places nowadays, Martha," I said solemnly. "Maybe you've heard of it. They're called airplanes. And Junior has a pilot's license. I checked this morning."

"Well, stone the crows." She stared at me thoughtfully. "I wonder if Sam knows that?"

"Don't know. Don't care." I said solidly. I did not intend to tell her about my phone call to his house.

"H-m-m. Did you call Captain Nordan?"

Yes, but he was already in surgery, and of course they wouldn't tell me why, or anything else. I'm going to be out until one at least," I said glancing at my watch. "Will you call later and see how he's doing? I'm going over to Windsor House with Birdie."

I told her why and told her what I wanted her to do about Cyndie Dancer and Berthe Anderson. "And one more thing," I said as she started out. "Have you located that other banker? I think his name was Peter something."

"Peter Newell. No, not yet, but I think I've got a line on him. I did find out one thing that might be significant, if what you're thinking about Junior is right. Both he and Junior belonged to the same country club, and played golf together on a regular basis."

Birdie picked me up at ten-thirty. We made the trip to Windsor in almost total silence. Birdie said she was too depressed to make conversation and I was afraid I'd give away what I knew no matter what I started out to say.

The hospital administrator, Dr. Bruce, met us at the main doors. He knew Birdie but said I would have to wait in the lounge as he could not discuss a patient with anyone except family.

Birdie lifted her normally soft little chin and said if he intended to discuss anything with her that morning he would have to do so in front of me. He set his mouth to disagree, took a good look at her expression and invited both of us into his office.

"This is highly irregular," he said wearily. "But I must talk to one of the family and I haven't been able to contact anyone in several days. No one has returned my calls."

"One of our family members was murdered Monday night and another was run down by a hit-run driver. We still don't know if she is going to live," Birdie said stiffly. "We haven't had time for anything but the essentials. I'm sorry."

He stared at her blankly. "I'm sorry. I didn't know. But, Miss Swallow, this is essential." He paused, took a deep breath, and apparently decided he would have to be as blunt as she was. "I'm also sorry to tell you that we cannot keep you grandmother in Windsor House any longer. And in the circumstances I'm afraid I will have to recommend Steilacoom."

Birdie gasped. "Steilacoom? Why?"

"Because this facility is not geared to take care of the criminally insane."

"But she's not," Birdie cried, jumping to her feet. "She's not a criminal and she's not insane. You know she isn't." For a moment they simply stared at each other then Birdie broke down in tears. She collapsed back into her chair and covered her face with her hands, her whole body shaking with grief and strain.

I stood, glaring at the man. "That was a thoroughly rotten way to tell her," I said hotly, patting Birdie's shoulder. "If you are any kind of a doctor you could see she was already stressed out, and she told you why."

He had the decency to look ashamed. "I'm sorry," he said. "I shouldn't have. . . . At the moment we are having a crisis of our own here, but I had no business. . . . I apologize, but the fact remains, other arrangements must be made for Mrs. Swallow. I—" The phone cut him off. He picked it up, his face blanching as he listened, then put it down carefully. "I'm sorry. I have to leave you for a bit. Would you like to wait in the lounge?"

"No. I want to see my Gran," Birdie said, tears still dripping.

He stopped, pursing his lips. "All right. I'll have some one escort you to her room," he said, ushering us out of his office.

"Here, wipe your face. You'll scare Rosellen," I told Birdie astringently as we were led down a long hall a few minutes later.

Birdie took my offered tissue and made a swipe at her face, smearing the mascara that had dribbled down her cheeks into horizontal streaks. "Hey, where are you go-ing?" she asked the attendant ahead of us. "My grand-mother isn't in this wing. She's on the main floor."

"No, she's in one of the rooms on this floor now," the woman said pleasantly, waving us through a metal de-tector that was set in the center of the hall and on through double gates that looked a lot like prison bars despite their ornamental curlicues.

We went past two closed doors and then into a small lounge where we were told to wait. A few minutes later the woman returned with Rosellen who greeted us both warmly, gave Birdie a kiss, and sat down on a davenport against the wall.

"What's the matter, dear? Why have you been crying?" she asked, patting the cushions beside her for Birdie to sit.

I remained standing by the window.

Birdie told her about Jane, surprising me a little. I wouldn't have upset her with anything like that. She murmured little sounds of sympathy but didn't seem to really take in what Birdie was telling her until Birdie said that she, Rosellen, wasn't to worry as Jane was going to be all right.

Birdie had her face down, her eyes on their entwined fingers, as she told her that so she didn't see the flash of expression that crossed Rosellen's face.

I did, and in that moment I knew.

Below me on the lawn I saw Dr. Bruce in earnest conversation with two other men and remembered Joey's comment. *"For a nuthouse it's sure a loose caboose."* Beyond the three men, through a screen of trees was a street corner. Two blocks further along a city bus was stopped at an intersection.

I excused myself and went back through the iron gates and down a back hall where I intercepted Dr. Bruce as he came in.

"I need to talk to you," I said quietly.

He looked at me vaguely, frowning, not recognizing me. "I'm sorry, not now. I have—"

"You've just located the route that one or more of your patients has been using as a private way out of this place," I interrupted.

That focused his attention with a snap.

Chapter Thirty

"Who are you?" he demanded.

"Nobody you need to worry about," I assured him. "But this is one time you'd better forget professional ethics and answer a few questions. I'm a private investigator and I'm investigating a murder."

The angry color drained out of his face. He didn't argue. He led the way back to his office and waved me to a chair before he sat down behind his desk. "All right, what do you want to know?" he asked.

"First, do you know who has been getting out and for how long?"

"No. We aren't even positive that anyone has. One of the staff simply found—"

"I don't need to know any more than that," I interrupted again. I was in a hurry. I didn't want Birdie to start wondering where I'd gone. "When did you decide you couldn't keep Rosellen Swallow here?"

He looked faintly surprised. He'd expected a more clinical question. "About six weeks ago. We informed Mr. Swallow and he said he'd make arrangements but we haven't heard from him since we allowed him to take his mother home on a visit." He made a wry grimace. "I think now that I shouldn't have done that, but . . ." He shrugged.

I started to ask who had done Rosellen's psychiatric evaluation but decided it didn't matter. "Has she been worse since she returned?" I asked instead.

"Yes, very agitated. That's why we moved her yesterday to our secure wing where she's under more constant observation."

Yesterday. Now I was sure.

I had a mental flashback to the file of records Jake had copied for me that first weekend. Everything had been there. Nothing had been glossed over, no line of investigation neglected. I'd simply spent time fishing in muddy water.

We left Windsor shortly after noon and Birdie took me back to the office, both of us as silent as before. It wasn't until we were within a block of my door that I remembered the diary and told her what I'd discovered. I thought it might amuse her.

I should have had better sense. Or at least waited until she stopped. She burst into tears again and came within an inch of hitting another car as she swerved into the parking lot behind the building.

"They aren't going to let her out, are they, Demary?" she sobbed. "The diary didn't mean a thing. They still think she killed Grandpa and Dian, don't they?"

"I'm afraid so," I said gently, feeling about as sorry as I've ever felt about anything in my life. I didn't tell her I was reasonably sure that her "Gran" had not only killed her husband and Dian, she had also stabbed Ruth Swallow and tried to kill Jane. Rosellen's charming facade covered a devious and violent personality. I was suddenly very glad she'd be in a more secure environment from now on.

A little later, still feeling miserable, I told Martha all that I knew, and, or, thought I knew. What I couldn't make up my mind on was what to do with the information.

"The whole family told me Rosellen was guilty. They were quite definite about it, I was just too stupid to listen," I said wearily.

"No, you believed Birdie, or wanted to, which amounted to the same thing," she said. "What I don't understand is how the family, or Junior, was able to swing the cover-up."

"Fairly simply is my guess. According to all the records there was never any physical evidence linking her to the murder. Nothing except the pipe and that was easily explained. It would have been a hard case to prove so the D.A. agreed to drop the prosecution if Rosellen was put away. Easier on everyone and Junior knew the right people to persuade."

"But how did she do it? She is simply too small to have lifted them into that big freezer."

"I think that's where the little pearl-handled gun came in. My guess is that she caught Howard and Dian embracing. She smacked him with the pipe and then put the gun to Dian's head. She forced her to carry him up to the shed and put him in the freezer, then cracked her one as she bent over to get him inside. She probably threw the gun in the sound, buried the bloody spread in the sand, and thought that would be the end of it."

Martha made a sour face. "And when they were found, a few dollars here, a few dollars there, the right word here, the right word there, and Bob's your uncle. Rosellen is in Windsor, not in Walla Walla where she belonged."

"That's about it. And I think that's what killed Ruth. Junior must have told the older members of the family of Dr. Bruce's decision and that's what he and Ruth were talking about the night I overheard them. Rosellen overheard them also and she misunderstood the same as I did. What she thought was that Ruth was going to blow the whistle, which would put her in Walla Walla for sure, so she sneaked out of Windsor Monday night and killed her. And then tried to kill Jane when they met at the intersection and Jane recognized her. Rosellen hadn't been in the neighborhood for twenty years and was probably lost, that's why the time lapse between when Mrs. Hollie saw her on Ruth's back porch and when she hit Jane."

"She stole the car?"

"Yes. I called Carol Ann a few minutes ago. The car was parked less than half a mile from Windsor. A spare set of keys was hidden under the driver's seat." I shook my head. "You would think the guy who owned it, an accomplished car thief, would know better than to do that, wouldn't you?"

I spent the next couple of hours getting everything I knew down on paper—actually into the computer—but I still couldn't decide what to do with the information. Telling all wasn't going to change anything as far as Rosellen was concerned but it would destroy Birdie, and wouldn't help the rest of the family either.

On the other hand, not telling anyone would mean a lot of tax dollars spent on a useless investigation. When, and if, Jane recovered consciousness she might identify her grandmother, or Sam would probably figure it out in the end, but to what purpose?

I was leaning back in my chair staring at the ceiling and still wrestling with the problem when Martha came in and nodded at the phone.

"Howard Junior is on the line. Said it was important that he speak to you."

"Did you tell him I was here?"

"No, but I think you'd better talk to him. He sounds . . . Talk to him."

I picked up my phone, uncertain and reluctant.

"Miss Jones, I need to see you," he said as soon as I spoke.

"Why? It won't change anything," I said, deciding to be as blunt as everyone else had been this morning.

"No, it won't," he said, sounding more annoyed than unhappy. "What I hoped to do was to persuade you not to go to the police with what you know. Dr. Bruce left me a message. He told me you had been at Windsor this morning." His voice hardened. "I knew you'd keep digging until you uncovered everything," he said, sounding angry now. "What good will it do you to make it all public?"

I hung up on him. He'd made up my mind for me.

I went over to the door and called Martha. "See if you can get Sam on the phone for me, will you?"

It would be an untidy end to an untidy story, but it wasn't my job to clean it up.

Epilogue

Rosellen Swallow was committed to Steilacoom three weeks later, without any publicity. As Sam said, there was no point in it.

I did check out Windsor House's record and found that twenty-two years ago it had been considered one of the leading psychiatric institutions in the state. It hadn't been, as I'd imagined, a luxury rest home.

Another thing I checked was under the edges of Martha's desk, and every other place I thought she might not have scrubbed after the little bag lady had left the office that day. I found three good prints—of Rosellen Swallow's. I couldn't even make a guess why she had risked coming but I was glad she couldn't do it again.

The Washington State Bar Association reprimanded Junior for unspecified wrongdoing but no action was taken. I'd been right about almost everything he'd done, just wrong about why he'd done it.

I haven't heard from Birdie since the day we went to Windsor House. She knows I'm not the one responsible for what happened, so maybe, someday, we will be friends again. I miss her.

Jane recovered and seems to be as good as new other than a blank spot in her memory. She doesn't remember anything between the time she left the tavern and when she finally recovered consciousness in the hospital.

Captain Nordan was operated on for a benign tumor and recovered speedily. He still wants me to go to Alaska. He said he'd even pay my passage on one of the luxury liners if it would hurry me on my way. I thought that was a great idea. I deserve a luxury trip.

I never did tell Sam what I'd thought about the beautiful brunette. I did find out who she was, though. Sam introduced her to me. She wasn't as young as she'd looked from a distance.

Nor, according to Martha, as beautiful as she looked to my jealous eyes.

She was Sam's second cousin, visiting from South Africa where she'd lived for the past twenty-five years. Sam had mentioned her any number of times, but how was I to know she looked like that soap-opera star?